**DEATH IN GOLD**

'Whitey threw the bottle that was close to his left hand and fell fast to his right. He heard the roar of the Mexican's gun, loud in the confined space of the cantina. He rolled and pushed himself up into a crouch, banging against another table as he did so. His Colt was drawn and clear and the first shot smacked into the centre of the Mex's crotch. There was a scream of pain and two more shots, one upon the other. The one that was Coburn's took another of the Mexicans high in the chest and sent him staggering back against the white wall, blood pumping through his shirt and staining his gun belt . . .'

Also in this series

HERNE THE HUNTER 1: WHITE DEATH
HERNE THE HUNTER 2: RIVER OF BLOOD
HERNE THE HUNTER 3: THE BLACK WIDOW
HERNE THE HUNTER 4: SHADOW OF THE VULTURE
HERNE THE HUNTER 5: APACHE SQUAW

and published by Corgi Books

John J. McLaglen

# Herne the Hunter
# 6: Death in Gold

CORGI BOOKS
A DIVISION OF TRANSWORLD PUBLISHERS LTD

HERNE THE HUNTER 6:
DEATH IN GOLD

A CORGI BOOK 0 552 10603 8

First publication in Great Britain

PRINTING HISTORY
Corgi edition published 1977

Copyright © 1977 by John J. McLaglen

Corgi Books are published by
Transworld Publishers Ltd.,
Century House, 61–63 Uxbridge Road,
Ealing, London W5 5SA
Made and printed in Great Britain by
Cox & Wyman Ltd., London, Reading and Fakenham

*For Tom Wild: a good and true friend*

## Chapter One

The sound of shattering glass cut jaggedly across the saloon. A chair scraped harshly as the figure of a young man backed away from one of the tables.

Heads turned, voices were raised then quickly lowered. Men began to move away from the bar, forming automatically the curve of a circle. In front of the ornately patterned mirror, the barkeep ducked his balding head as his hands reached for the scatter gun stashed in case of trouble. Halfway there he stopped: he knew the reputation of the man still sitting at the table. He wasn't about to get involved. Likely wouldn't need to.

'You got no call to say that.' The kid sounded even younger when he spoke, his voice high-pitched and thin.

He had stopped backing away and stood his ground in a slight forward crouch, his right hand hovering close to the butt of his revolver.

'No call.'

The watching crowd was silent, almost without movement. Behind the onlookers a hobbling shape, no more than four foot in height, moved awkwardly but quickly, greedily draining the unattended glasses.

'You take that back or I'll ram those words down your damned throat with this gun barrel!'

'I doubt that, son.'

The voice was slow, strong. The speaker was still half-covered by the shadows at the corner of the room.

The youngster's fingers grazed the edge of his gun butt. 'Don't call me son – old man!' he sneered.

The man at the table moved his chair back with his body, careful to keep both hands well in sight. He stood up and walked round the table with what might have been a brief sigh of regret. But at no time did his eyes waver or his concentration falter.

'Seems to me nothin' I said 'd rightly make you so all-fired touchy. Why don't you step over t' the bar and we'll have us a drink an' no hard feelings?'

The kid took another half pace and shook his head. 'You ain't gonna talk your way out of this, old man. Not like that you ain't. Not after what you said.'

'All I said was, I didn't think you was much with that thing you got strapped to your side there.'

'How the hell you know that? You ain't even seen me.'

A flicker of a smile showed on the gunfighter's lined face, then disappeared as quickly as the sun on a late autumn afternoon.

'Damn it, boy, I seen kids like you from here till doomsday. You ain't no different from the rest of 'em.'

'That's a lie! You're a rotten, stinkin' liar!'

The kid's fingers stretched and arched. The men at the front of the curve of watchers shifted back, elbows pushing into those behind. The barkeep lifted the full bottles down from the bar and slipped them out of harm's way. The dwarf threw back his disproportionately large head and swallowed down the remnants of another glass of whiskey, his eyes already beginning to bulge from their sockets.

The man stepped fully into the light. He was almost two inches over six foot and weighed around two hundred pounds. His hair was dark and long, reaching towards his broad shoulders, greying at the temples: it had been greying for some years now. A Colt .45 hung below his right hip. The plain walnut grip shone dully with use; the curved tip of the hammer picked up a reflection from the light overhead and flashed out a sudden star. A star eclipsed by the man's hand.

Jedediah Travis Herne. He had killed his first man in eighteen fifty-nine. Now it was eighteen eighty-three and the killing hadn't stopped. Men called him Herne the Hunter.

'All right, son. I'll give you a chance to prove me wrong.'

There was an audible intake of breath from those gathered round, followed by a further shift towards the edges and door of the saloon. The dwarf climbed up on to the far end of the long bar and sat with his legs dangling, eyes large and red and gleaming.

Herne moved his left hand cautiously up to the pocket at the front of his black waistcoat and ducked finger and thumb inside. Both the youngster and the crowd watched him, mesmerised.

He drew out a silver coin and held it up in front of his face.

'What the hell's that for?'

'You want to prove yourself, don't you?'

'I don't see how . . .'

'Shut up and listen! When I drop this coin, you go for that gun of yorn. We'll see how fast you are.'

The kid swung his head fractionally to one side; his eyes narrowed and a bubble of saliva appeared at one corner of his mouth.

'Don't you try to make a fool of me! I didn't come here to play no damn games. If'n I'm gonna prove myself then we'll face up like men.'

Herne tossed the coin into the air with his left hand and caught it once more.

'Make up your mind, boy. I ain't about to waste a lot more time on you.'

The coin disappeared in the centre of the large, strong hand, Herne's eyes were fixed on the kid's, coldly and dispassionately. He would rather not kill him as long as there was a choice. Only the way the boy was prodding him there soon wouldn't be any choice at all.

Which would be too bad for the kid.

Herne glanced at the gun at the boy's side. The belt was slung too low, the holster a couple of inches further down the thigh than it needed to be for a fast, curving draw. The revolver was a Remington Frontier .44. It was a close model of Herne's own Peacemaker Colt, but inferior. The balance was out – not by a whole lot, but enough. In a gunfight, the merest fraction was enough.

'What's it goin' t' be, son?'

The head twitched again, involuntarily. At the other end of the saloon, the dwarf started to sing a tuneless, incoherent song, his deformed legs swinging from side to side in time.

Herne tossed the coin a final time.

'Okay. Play your fool game.'

'Uh-huh.'

Herne turned sideways, left arm extended, silver coin clearly visible between the tips of finger and thumb.

'I ain't gonna toss it, just let it fall. Soon as it leaves my hand you go for your gun. You got that?'

'Sure I got it. Plain enough, ain't it?'

The crowd began to edge forward once more, whispering and nudging, leaning on the shoulders of others or clambering on to chairs and tables for a better view. The barkeep measured the distance between himself and his scatter gun. Just in case things get out of hand.

Herne lifted his hand a couple of inches before his fingers parted and the bright coin fell to the scuffed and dirty floor.

The kid clawed for his pistol, dragging it upwards desperately, thumb pulling back on the hammer.

In the fresh and expectant silence, the coin hit the wooden board, wavered, spun round in a tight circle, wobbled and was still.

The youngster looked at the coin, then up at Herne. Colour flooded his cheeks and his mouth opened wide. His tongue licked excitedly at his upper lip.

'Damn me!' shouted one of the onlookers. 'The boy done it! He cleared leather before the piece hit the floor.'

'Sure did! Good a draw as I seen fer a long time.'

'Was that. Never reckoned he could have done it.'

'No, sir.'

The dwarf had tucked his legs up under his squat body and was perched on the bar, singing louder, more tunelessly than ever.

The kid took a couple of steps towards Herne, the Remington still tight in his right hand, the hammer still cocked back. Herne's own hand rested on the butt of his Colt, ready.

'See that, old man? See me draw afore that damned coin of yorn could drop? You ain't gonna tell me that weren't fast.'

Herne watched the boy's fingers on his gun. 'Now you just ease back that hammer, before you do anything else.'

'Not till you admit that was fast. Faster 'n you figured I'd be.'

'Okay, boy. You was fast. Faster than I thought. Now will you ease that damned thing back?'

The kid flushed even more brightly and half-turned to look at the crowd, which was still murmuring its approval. His thumb gently released the hammer and slid the gun back into its holster.

'Buy you a drink afore you head out of here?' said Herne.

'What you mean, head out of here? You just said how fast I was.'

Herne stared at him. 'You're fast, right enough. Trouble is, you just ain't fast enough.'

The boy spread his gun hand once more, the colour draining from his cheeks. Some of the crowd called out their disbelief but Herne stood his ground.

'Ain't no one faster 'n that. Not with that coin trick. Not even you.'

'Go home, boy. You done well. Go home and practice.

Maybe you'll get better.' If'n you don't get dead, Herne added to himself, if'n you don't get dead first.

The crowd pressed further forward; the kid took another step towards the central light.

'You do it.' he taunted. 'You show how it can be done faster.'

Herne nodded his head slowly, then called to the bartender. 'That gun you bin eyin' under there. You care to lift it up so's we can all see?'

'Sure.'

The bald man moved down the bar and pulled the scatter gun up into sight.

'Now cock both barrels and steady it against the counter, real easy.'

Beads of sweat formed on the barkeep's rounded forehead; every eye was upon him. Every eye but Herne's. He was watching the kid in front of him.

'Right?'

'Right, Mister Herne. Plumb proud to help out anyways I...'

'Save the talk. Just keep that thing so that it covers anyone who might want to grab a part of the action. I don't aim to leave myself without shells and no back-up. You understand me?'

The barkeep gulped his understanding as Herne crossed his left hand to his holster and pulled out the Colt as carefully as he had lifted the silver coin from his pocket. Holding it high so that everyone could see, he ejected the shells on to the floor, where they bounced and rolled in all directions only stopping when they came up against a gap in the boards, the leg of a table, a mound of sawdust – the boot of the disbelieving kid opposite.

'Take up the coin, son.'

'I told you not to call me that!'

'Take up the coin!'

Herne spun the empty chamber of the Colt. The boy hesitated a moment longer then scooped up the coin.

'Hold it high so's folks can see.'

The kid glowered but did as he was told. Even the dwarf had stilled now. Everyone watched expectantly, wondering what more the ageing gunfighter could so.

Once more the coin reflected a whorl of light from its silver surface; the youngster twitched his head, then pulled his fingers from the coin as though it had burnt his skin.

In the silence of the saloon Herne the Hunter swooped for his gun, left arm thrust out at an angle for balance. The hammer clicked audibly down on an empty chamber: once: twice. And then came the metallic clink of coin against wood.

The silence held for five, almost ten seconds. Then voices rose in amazement, in delight and noisy acclamation. The barkeep wiped the sweat from his forehead with the sleeve of his white shirt and slowly let back the hammers of his gun. At the end of the bar the dwarf bobbed up and down and pretended to play a tune on an empty bottle, holding it as if it were a flute.

Only the kid made neither movement nor sound.

The gunfighter had been able to draw and fire twice in the time it had taken him simply to pull his gun clear and begin the motions of his first shot.

He stared at the coin, still now in the circle of light, and the shells scattered around it. Twice, his brain kept telling him, repeating it over and over. Twice. He made it twice.

'What's the matter, kid?' someone shouted from the middle of the group of watchers. 'You lose somethin'?'

'Damn right he did!'

'Not such a fire cracker now, is he?'

Herne stepped over to the youngster and looked at the now pale face, the lingering disbelief in the eyes. 'Want that drink, son?'

The head twitched sharply and the kid turned on his heel, pushing his way through the crowd whose cheers had turned to jeers. Then there were men pushing forward with the stink of stale beer on their breaths and empty compliments on their tongues. They wanted to shake the stranger's hand, to clap him on the back; even to lay a finger on the shiny butt of the gun he had drawn with such speed.

'Here, mister. Here's your shells.'

Herne accepted them from the trembling hands of a willowy saloon girl with dark curly hair and a sad, uncertain smile. No more than a kid. He knew her also; girls like her. They were all over the West, working every cathouse and bar that would take them. Until their bodies became riddled with disease or just plain ugly and ill-used. Then they found somewhere quiet and private and waited to die.

Herne looked back at the girl's face and didn't smile. She turned from him with a toss of her hair. Herne reloaded his gun, then walked over to the bar.

'That was mighty fine gunplay, Mister Herne. Knew you was good 'cause of your reputation, but never reckoned on anything like that. No, sir. Not like that.'

The bald man started to sweat again, his hands polishing on a glass so energetically that it looked ready to break.

'Thanks for your help with that scatter gun of yorn.'

The barkeep set down the glass and beamed. 'That weren't nothin'. Anytime you want. I'd be only too pleased to stand up alongside a man like you. Yes, sir, Mister Herne, somethin' to feel right proud of. Somethin' to tell my kids about when they've gotten a mite older.'

'How in Hell's name you gonna tell your kids anythin', Walt, you don't even know where half of 'em are!'

The cowboy at Herne's right banged his bottle hard on the bar top and roared with laughter at his own joke. In the middle of the laughter came another sound, a jagged, jangly singing, excited and high. As Herne turned to face it, the sound cut off and was replaced by a voice which squealed: 'Don't move!'

The gunfighter tensed, stopped. Nerves, muscles alert, ready.

'Got me a gun of my own. Pointin' right up to your back. Can't miss from here.'

Herne turned round slowly. The dwarf was standing close to the side of the bar, an old Navy Colt held tightly in both hands. The effort of holding it steady was evident in the tightness of the arms, the bulge of the huge forehead, the eyes protruding from their sockets so far that they looked ready to burst free.

'What you gonna do now, mister?'

The voice squeaked its question, then lapsed back into its tuneless song. Herne was aware of the stillness in the long room, the distance from his hand to the Colt at his side, the effort the dwarf was making to keep the gun pointing upwards at his chest. And then, from the corner of his eye, he noticed the barkeep sliding slowly down behind his counter, hands reaching underneath it as he did so.

The dwarf noticed nothing; continued with his song, pleasure dancing across his straining eye-balls.

'Hap!'

Despite himself, the dwarf swivelled round at the sudden sound of his name. His face met the swing of the scatter gun, the heavy butt smashing into it with all of the barkeep's strength.

There was a crunching of bone and a scream sharp as the point of a needle. The end of the big gun came up and down once more. This time the sickening thud of wood on bared bone echoed round the saloon and the dwarf collapsed to the floor.

Herne slipped his Colt back into its holster and bent down quickly, lifting up the dropped revolver and passing it across the bar to the bald man whose grin was spread broader than ever.

'You better look after this. And thanks. Saved me having to kill the poor bastard.'

'Hell, that were nothin'. Least I could do. He ain't but half a man anyways. Damned fool that he is.'

Some of the customers picked up the dwarf and laid him on one of the tables, so that his feet just hung over the edge. His head lolled to one side, seeming even less a part of his body than usual. The wide nose was bloody and pushed to one side; the one eye that was visible hung oddly downwards on to his battered face.

The barkeep passed Herne a whiskey bottle and a glass and the gunfighter poured himself a good tot and drank it down in a single swallow.

He nodded to the man behind the bar and began to move away but he was called back. The bald head leaned over the counter. 'That right what you said? You'd have bothered killin' a nothin' like Hap?'

Herne looked back at the man with cold, unwavering eyes. 'Knew a man once, down Lincoln County way. Billy Bonny, least that's what he was christened. Said to me one time, "Jed, when you're the fastest it ain't the second fastest you got to worry about most, nor the third. It's the fifty-first. The one you don't know. The one you can't work out. The one as might do any damned thing. That's when you need to be real careful and take the least chances." '

Herne stood up straight. 'Longest damned speech Billy ever made, least in my hearing. But sure was sense.' He looked at the changing expression in the barkeep's eyes. 'I'd have killed him right enough. Before he could've pulled back the trigger on that old thing he'd have been plumb dead.'

He coughed and spat down into the wide rim of the cuspidor alongside the bar. 'Poor bastard!'

Jed Herne walked briskly across the main street. For one thing the nights were getting colder. For another he knew better than to linger in that open space. The lights from the saloon would mark out his shadow as he stepped towards the softer light which showed in the doorway of the hotel where he had a room.

He pushed open the door and walked across the threadbare carpet and up the bare boards of the single flight of stairs. He was tired; the bed would feel good under him. A mattress of straw was better than a blanket on the ground.

Huh! Herne smiled ruefully to himself as he turned the key in the lock. Was a time when I would've thought that was real soft.

He stepped through into the darkness and as he did so he heard clearly, like hammers on the brain, the triple click of a gun being cocked.

## Chapter Two

Jed Herne froze. Mouth slightly opened, breath half drawn. Inside his head a clock ticked away the seconds as the shadows began to reveal the outlines of a shape. He could not see the gun, but he could guess where it was. His own right hand was snaking downwards, cautious and deadly as a rattler preparing to strike.

The shape shifted.

'Jed?'

The harsh, metallic tick of time in Herne's brain was replaced by a flash of recognition, then a cold shiver of shock the full length of his spine. But Coburn was . . . dead!

'Whitey?'

The room seemed to be getting lighter with every moment; the shape took on form, features. Herne saw the outline of the gun; watched as it was holstered. Saw the snow-white hair, the face of the albino. A face in which only the eyes were as yet unclear.

Herne had no need to see the eyes to know them. He was unlikely to forget. Where the blood vessels of the iris showed through, they shone pinkly through the snow of the man's face.

The man who had long been his friend.

The man who had taken a contract to kill him.

Isaiah 'Whitey' Coburn.

Few men called him Whitey and lived to speak the name twice. Herne was one of these. He steadied his shaken nerves and asked, a tone almost of outrage in his voice, 'Hell, Whitey. What game you playin'?'

'No game, Jed. Can't a man stop by to see a friend when he's a mind?'

'Sure. Only some folk might think it a strange way to go visitin' friends.'

'Can't be too careful these days, Jed. You know that probably better 'n' me.'

Coburn stifled what might have been a chuckle or a cough. Herne could see the pink eyes now, the lean white face above the slim, wiry body.

'Seems to me your hand's still mighty close to that Colt of yorn, Jed.'

Herne nodded. 'Seems to me the last time we met you was takin' dollars for puttin' a bullet in my hide.'

This time it was a snort of laughter, harsh and short. 'That's right enough.'

'That still the case?'

'No more.'

'How come?'

Coburn looked up at the man who had been his friend for more years than he cared to remember. 'Money ran out. Money that was payin' me. Heard tell you put a shell into old man Nolan's brain and all his hard-earned money just ran out along of the blood. Seemed to me that when that happened, my contract was finished. Terminated.'

Herne's fingers moved inches further from his gun.

'Speakin' of terminated, Whitey, I thought that's what you were. Didn't reckon on seein' you agin this side of the Divide.'

Coburn spread his hands wide. 'Hell, Jed. That weren't nothin'.'

'As I remember it was by the Rich Stream Falls and they was all iced over like some fancy wedding cake. You took a leap while we was fightin' and your heel skidded on the ice. Nothin' but the moon to see by an' that was covered by cloud most of the time. Last I saw of you was your arms flailin' fit to bust. Last I heard was four words risin' up from the darkness.'

'What words was those, Jedediah?'

'Far as I recall they was "Son of a bitch".'

Whitey Coburn stood up and laughed aloud. He stepped towards Herne and clasped him by both arms, holding him in a firm grip.

'Thank the Lord for that,' he said. 'I'd have been plumb unhappy if'n I'd thought of goin' t' my death with a prayer on my lips. Happen that was what saved me. They do say the Devil looks after his own.'

Herne grinned back. 'They surely do say that.'

'Son of a bitch!' said Coburn softly. 'Son of a bitch.'

Fifteen minutes later the two men were sitting in front of the small wood fire that Herne had lit in the grate. Coburn had produced from his pocket a bottle of Jim Beam best Kentucky Bourbon and they were sitting back warming their bodies with the fire and their throats with the alcohol.

In a life where there had been little trust, little true friendship, Herne was glad for such a moment.

'Heard you got yourself a job,' drawled Coburn as the contents of the bottle gradually decreased.

'Right enough.'

'An' you're lookin' for men.'

'Yep.'

Coburn cleared his throat and spat down into the fire. The ball of spittle struck the underside of a log, sending up a jet of hissing and crackling green flame. 'Had any luck?'

'No. Some've tried. Weren't good enough.'

Whitey Coburn said nothing, merely nodded.

Herne pushed at the edge of a log with his boot. 'An old timer with one arm and a couple of kids, that's all there's been.'

'Uh-huh. Figures.' Coburn reached for the bottle and poured them both another shot. It sure was a good place to be! Damn well was!

He leaned towards Herne and studied Jed's face in the flickering light of the fire. Not all that long ago he'd been doing his level best to lodge a bullet in it. Nothing personal, though, a job of work like any other. And Coburn's work, like Herne's, was with a gun; like Jed, he treated his work seriously.

'Don't forget we was kids once,' Coburn reminded him.

'I know it. Thought about it earlier this evenin'. Boy come in the saloon, fresh-faced, young. Likely saved all his money from workin' on the farm t' buy hisself a gun. Practiced Sunday mornings stead of goin' t' church.'

'He not practiced enough?'

'Not yet. Maybe not ever. Reckon he's comin 'twenty already. You an' me, we'd done our share of shootin' by then.'

'Too damn right!' Coburn drained his glass and poured in some more. 'Way I recall, we was both around eighteen when we was riding with that bastard Quantrill.'

'Jesus Christ! William Clarke Quantrill! That would have been round the time that kid back in the saloon was born.'

'Whole lot happened since then.'

Herne looked at the bottle of bourbon, at the orange light refracted through the almost empty glass. 'Still ain't no way I'm goin' t' forget it. Little more 'n' a month afore my nineteenth birthday we rode into Lawrence.'

He kicked out at the fire again, sending sparks and smoke high up into the chimney, staring absently into the flare of flame.

'Lawrence, Kansas.' He mused.

. . . Out of the dark centre of Herne's memory a woman ran towards him. Her arms were stretched wide in a gesture of appeal. He could see the wide brown eyes fixed upon him, saw the mouth open but was unable to hear the words she uttered. They were lost in the general atmosphere of terror and destruction that filled the air.

As she came alongside his horse's flanks, he noticed a small scar on her right cheek. One detail picked from so many – yet he had never forgotten it. The scar, the brown eyes, the back of her dress on fire, burning her body.

Her hand had briefly touched his leg, then she had plummeted suddenly backwards as though struck by some invisible fist. Herne had watched her roll over on her back, screeching in pain. The flames had been quenched but by then it was too late. A bullet, one of many that were flying through the air at the time, had penetrated her neck and ploughed out through her throat.

After the massacre, Quantrill claimed that no women had been killed. He might even have believed it. But in that bloody, burning holocaust it was impossible to tell whether the running figures were man or woman, adult or child.

... Herne had felt something tugging at the bridle of his mount, trying to turn it. He had lashed out with his boot. Once. Twice. The third blow had freed the attacker's grip and sent him sprawling on the dirt of the main street. Herne pulled his pistol from its holster. His first shot went wide and he cursed the awkward heavy action of the gun, a double-action Tranter .44, one of a number imported by the Confederacy from Britain.

It did its work the second time. The form on the ground jerked into an acute spasm of agony, half of its face blown away. When Herne stared down at what remained he realized he had just killed a boy of little more than eleven or twelve years old.

... Coburn was being dragged from the saddle and set upon with lengths of wood, iron pans, a butcher's knife. Herne had ridden hard into the midst of the crowd, the rebel yell loud on his youthful lips and his curved sabre held high above his head. He had taken it from the corpse of a Union lieutenant after a group of Quantrill's men had ambushed them a week before.

As the butcher's knife came down dangerously close to his friend's face, Herne plunged the sabre blade downwards, slicing through flesh and sheering bone.

Through his vision a bespectacled face now loomed out at him and he saw once more the edge of the sabre as it split the nose in two as neatly and precisely as meat on a wooden block. The blood had spurted high enough to dapple his uniform trousers and the saddle of his horse.

Then Whitey had been smiling at him as he clambered up on to a riderless mount and wheeled it round, heading for the thick of the fray.

... And all the time the smoke had got thicker, darker, causing the lungs to cough up acrid bile and the eyes to water and smart. The fire had sped from timber to timber so that eventually it had been akin to fighting a battle in the midst of Hell.

... A white-haired old man with three bullet wounds in a diagonal line across his chest, wandering aimlessly about amongst the carnage. Singing hymns.

... A mother sheltering in the rear of a blazing building, her arms spread over her two children like a mother hen about its chicks. She need not have bothered; both were dead already.

... Slowly dragging himself along the edge of the boardwalk, a Union soldier, a straight-bladed 'Prussian' cavalry sabre embedded in his spine.

... The screams of an old woman who turned suddenly towards Herne, her hands holding her breast as it fell forwards from her chest, only a thin flap of skin still unsevered.

... Lawrence, Kansas. The twenty-first of January, 1863. The birth of Quantrill's raiders. There was no way in which either Jed Herne or Whitey Coburn would forget it – their baptism of fire.

Herne shifted in his chair and blinked around the still

darkening room. The flames were duller now, the atmosphere colder. He looked at Whitey alongside him, eyes closed in sleep or perhaps lost in his own thoughts, who could tell? The bottle of Jim Beam lay on its side by his foot, empty.

'Herne! Herne the Hunter! We know you're up there.'

The voice cut through Jed's thoughts and he was instantly awake and alive; back in the present. A gunman who was older than perhaps he had any right to be, certainly better than most of his contemporaries who were now dead. Maybe that was why he was still alive.

But there were always those around who would do their best to change things.

'Herne! You get down here and face us out! Less'n you're afraid!'

Herne stood up and automatically tested the weight of his Colt. Coburn was alert now, waiting for his partner's lead.

'What's the matter old man? It past your bed time?'

Coburn looked up at Herne questioningly as the last remark was greeted by raucous, drunken laughter from outside in the street.

'This'll wake the old bastard up!'

'A volley of gunshots cracked out, followed by more whooping and yelling.

'Seems,' said Coburn laconically, 'as though you've got company.'

Herne grinned ruefully: 'Happen you're right.'

'Friends of yorn?'

Herne edged back the curtain and glanced downwards. 'Not exactly.'

'Come on, Herne. You ain't gonna show me up this time.'

Herne let the tattered curtain fall back into place. 'Thought so. It's that damned kid from the saloon. I didn't reckon his pride'd let him sit that one out. He's been back to the ranch or wherever 'n' got hisself some drinking partners. Soon as they got enough inside 'em, they rode back into town.'

Another shot rang out and Herne looked down on the street. Quite a crowd was gathering along the opposite side, outside the saloon. At its centre he recognized the bald bartender, his scatter gun resting across his left arm, right hand around the butt. He was looking up at the window of Herne's room.

'How many?' Coburn asked.

'Six. All with the cradle marks fresh off their fool arses.'

'What you reckon on doin'?'

'Damned if I know. Blasted fools might holler themselves out of if it I let 'em keep it up for long enough.'

Coburn raised a white eyebrow in disbelief.

Herne nodded slowly. 'I don't think so either.'

Down below the barkeep was talking to the youngster who had made his play against the silver coin. They spoke for several minutes, both gesturing and shaking their head in turn.

When the discussion was over, the bald man turned hastily away and went into the hotel. A few moments later he was knocking on the door of the room.

'It ain't locked.'

The man stepped quickly inside, careful to keep the weapon he was carrying down at his side.

'Walt, ain't it?' asked Herne.

'Yes, sir, Mister Herne.'

'They send you up here?' he pointed towards the window.

'Hell, no. Kids like that ain't goin' t' send me anywheres. Why, you saw in the saloon how I deal . . .'

Herne held up his hand. 'Sure. Sure. What's your piece?'

'I tried to talk 'em out of it' He looked from Herne to Coburn and back again, scarcely marking Whitey's albino face and hair. A bartender learns not to react to such things; it isn't good for business.

'And?'

'They won't shift. Say that if you don't come out, they'll shoot up the hotel and anyone who gets in their way and tries to stop 'em.'

Coburn checked the cartridges in his Colt. 'If they're no more than you say, there must be folk in town to stop them.'

The bald head shook from side to side. 'No sheriff here in town. Least, not a live one. Can't see no one else making a stand – not in a quarrel that ain't rightly their's.'

'Meaning its ours?' asked Herne.

'Well, Mister Herne, it's you they're after. Your name they're callin' yonder.'

Herne nodded and glanced at Whitey.

'If you an' your friend showed in the street, likely that would be enough to sober 'em to their goddamn senses.'

Coburn slid his gun into its holster. 'An' if it don't?'

The shouting from outside grew louder, angrier.

'I could take 'em a message,' said the bartender hopefully.

'All right, Walt. You tell 'em to give us a couple of minutes. We'll be down.'

The sweat shone on the man's head and the dull yellow of his teeth showed in a late flare from the dying coals in the grate. He turned and let himself out of the room.

'You don't have to get into this, Whitey,' said Herne, as he checked his own .45. 'Ain't your fight.'

Coburn grinned: 'Don't seem to be nothin' better to do. Fire's goin' out, bottle's empty. Too soon to go to sleep.'

There was a hasty knock and the hotel door opened again to show Walt's face peering round it.

'Your friend,' he said, gesturing at Coburn, 'he as fast as you are, Mister Herne?'

Herne hesitated a second, then gave a grim smile. 'Don't know for sure, but I do know one thing – I sure as hell wouldn't like to live on the difference.'

## Chapter Three

The waning moon was obscured by clouds that drifted carelessly across it. The lights of the saloon spilled out through the batwing doors and on to the hard, dirt street. An oil lamp showed in the window above the general store, a few buildings to the right. One of the tight group of spectators held a hurricane lamp high in the night air.

The bartender ducked out of the hotel, looked hastily around, then scurried over to his saloon, stopping alongside the entrance and breathing heavily. Before he could steady himself, the leader of the gang of drunken youngsters grabbed him by the collar.

'What'd he say?'

Walt moved his head to one side and brushed the hand away. He tightened his grasp of the scatter gun. 'Who the hell d'you think you're gettin' hold of?'

The kid lifted his knee into the man's crotch hard and fast, while his left hand reached down and took hold of his wrist; his right moved to his belt and came up with a Remington until the end of the barrel was alongside Walt's temple. The anger in the youngster's eyes was clear and frightening.

Walt knew nothing would stop the boy now: he would kill if he could. And the bartender didn't intend it should be him.

'All right,' he said, hastily. 'Take it easy. It's okay. He's comin'. *They're* comin'. Two of them.'

The pistol pushed harder against the man's head.

'Two? What two?'

'Friend of the gunfighter's. He was up there with him. Don't know anything else.'

The kid moved the gun away, but kept hold of the wrist. 'You sure they're comin' out?'

Walt nodded and as he did so the light in the front room of the hotel went out. Herne and the albino weren't going to set themselves up in silhouette; they knew better than that.

The kid saw the change in Walt's expression and turned his head to follow his stare.

'They're on their way!' he shouted to his friends.

'The gun,' he gestured to Walt.

The bartender shook his head; only once. This time the length of the kid's gun barrel cracked against the side of his head, instantly drawing blood. He stumbled backwards into the saloon wall.

'I said the gun!'

Walt wiped at the line of blood running freely down his cheek and lifted up the scatter gun, butt first. Like he'd already thought, he wasn't going to be the one to slake the kid's thirst for killing.

The boy swivelled round, his pistol holstered, the scatter gun pointing towards the front of the hotel opposite. Neither Herne nor Coburn had appeared.

'Keep watch!' he shouted. 'Get spread out! Don't make it any too easy for the bastards!'

He spat on to the boards beneath his feet and waited, straining his eyes into the darkness.

He took a step forward and opened his mouth to yell once more.

There was no need.

The moon slid out from behind a cloud and revealed the tall, thin figure of Jed Herne. His Colt was holstered at his right side and he didn't appear to be carrying any other weapon.

Of the second man, Whitey Coburn, there was no sign.

As the kid hesitated, Herne looked around, eyes narrowed beneath dark brows. Up on the sidewalk he could see the one from the saloon, the one who had been making most of the noise. And he had the barkeep's gun – that was something he had not reckoned with. A gun like that could do a powerful lot of damage.

The others were out in the street itself. There was a knot of three to his left, one tall youngster whose blond hair showed up clearly, two shorter, darker boys on either side of him. All three were armed with pistols as yet holstered by their sides. The tall one had a rifle held in his left hand. A .44 Winchester carbine, its twenty inch barrel not the most efficient for that kind of shootout.

The last pair were well separated, which made things more difficult. A fat boy who looked little more than fifteen or sixteen in the moonlight that illuminated his face, stood with feet splayed outwards, arms tight against his bulging sides. He gripped a sawed-off 12-gauge shotgun as though his life depended on it. Which, of course, it did. And so did Herne's.

The last one had his right leg bound in splints and rested that side of his tall, rangy body on a hefty wooden crutch. He had a Colt .45 in his left hand it was halfway from its holster, waiting for Herne to make his move.

They were all waiting for Herne to make his move.

The gunfighter knew they would not wait long. Untrained, unused to such situations, one of them would break. A gun would be jerked up and into action and after that moment there would be no let-up until it was all over.

Herne glanced quickly up at the sky. A line of cloud had slid across the face of the moon: there would be more to follow. He looked at the kid on the boardwalk and again wondered if there was any chance of talking him out of it.

And again he knew there was not.

It was the fair haired boy whose nerve snapped first. Right then, before the moon was covered. He brought the barrel of his Winchester down and round in Herne's direction. He never got the chance to pull the trigger.

Herne drew his Colt .45 and shot him through the head. The shell split the skull directly below the wave of light hair. Even before he had had time to rock backwards under the impact, Herne had fired again.

Swivelling to his right, he aimed at the kid with the scatter gun. He was a fraction late. The bullet tore through the youngster's coat sleeve and grazed his arm as he jumped to one side.

Herne dived for the dirt and rolled to his left, knowing the contents of the scatter gun might empty in his direction. What he heard instead was the single sharp bark of Coburn's Colt. Coming round from the rear of the hotel and into the street beyond the six kids, Whitey had had plenty of time to grab his share of the action.

He fancied the fat boy with the shotgun. Fancied him so much that he let him have two bullets all to himself. The first hammered into his left side. After the boy had thrown the shotgun away in his agony, Coburn got himself a better view of his face. In that kind of light faces presented the best target.

Coburn's second shot drove home inches behind the left eye socket and exited upwards at an angle through the brain.

'Bastard!' The kid on the boardwalk allowed himself to be distracted by Coburn's sudden appearance. He swung the scatter gun round sharply and fired both barrels. Whitey was no longer there. He had ducked back into the protecting darkness and started off for the front of the hotel in an easy run.

Herne was on one knee to the left of the hotel door, Colt steady in his hand. The first of the two short kids did his best to pull his gun clear of his holster. His best was nowhere near good enough.

Herne had plenty of time to place his shot and allowed himself a quick smile of satisfaction as the shell struck home at the left side of the kid's chest, no more than an inch from the centre of his heart.

Herne shifted the gun a fraction to the right. The second of the pair was reaching for the discarded Winchester. Herne's bullet pierced the flesh of his left shoulder and propelled him backwards. He had half rolled, half stumbled to his feet when Coburn's bullet entered at the base of his throat, smashing away his adam's apple and causing a sudden jet of blood to spurt upwards, where it was caught dramatically in the lamplight.

Four down: just the leader and the cripple remaining.

A shot dug into the dirt close enough to Coburn's right boot to make him hop involuntarily to the other side. Another streaked through the air and thudded into the hotel wall behind him.

Coburn raised his Colt but Herne touched his arm and indicated for him to hold his fire.

'No,' he said quickly, then ran across the street towards the saloon.

The boy with the crutch had got through the bat-wing doors seconds before him. Herne pushed hard into his back, sending his sprawling forward, vainly trying to keep his balance. As he toppled sideways towards one of the tables, a couple of shots flew past Herne's head from the direction of the bar.

Herne drew and fired in a blur of continuous movement. The bullet whistled over the kid's hastily ducked head and cracked the long ornamental mirror close to its centre. A section of glass fell forward and smashed into fragments on the floor behind the bar.

Herne ran low for the near end of the long counter, partly aware that the cripple was once more pushing himself to his feet but concentrating on the kid who had set everything in motion.

Now it was due to be finished: one way or the other.

A further piece of glass, long and jagged, slowly fell away

from the mirror and broke into a myriad silvered shards. The kid eased his gun along the edge of the bar and waited for Herne to show himself.

Herne reached forward and picked up a full bottle of beer. He lobbed it through the air, so that it landed behind the boy at the far end. Then Herne showed himself, and fast. He vaulted on to the counter, legs spread for balance, Colt drawn and in front of him. The smashing of the bottle was lost in the roar of the .45.

The kid blinked his startled eyes and gripped the bar rail with his left hand. Herne could see the knuckles whiten with the strain as the kid struggled to hold himself steady. Steady enough to stand and try to bring his own gun to bear. Herne waited until the kid's arm was almost level and then aimed and fired above it.

The shell ripped into the arm at the shoulder blade and the Remington clattered down on to the surface of the bar and skidded out of reach.

The kid's head gave a last, violent twitch and a gout of blood gushed from between his pale lips and splashed downwards. The left hand lost its grip and the kid pitched forwards, his hair falling into a pool of his own blood.

Herne watched and waited as the body slipped slowly backwards and thudded on to the sawdust strewn floor. Then he jumped down and walked along behind the bar towards where the kid had fallen.

It had been short enough time, but sufficient for him to have lost sight of the cripple. He was standing over the kid's dead body when Coburn shouted a warning from the doorway. Jed Herne swung his body low and round, drawing his Colt from its holster in the same movement.

The pistol levelled at him was already cocked. That being the case, Herne wasn't too dissatisfied that his shot missed the forehead and entered the face between cheekbone and jawbone, splintering the latter savagely.

It probably would not have killed him outright: he would

have taken hours to die. Mercy then that Whitey Coburn's bullet had struck the centre of his spine. He was dead before the pain in his face could register. His gun fell to the floor, unfired.

Coburn shrugged his shoulders. 'Didn't seem worth the risk,' he said apologetically. 'Not a nothin' like that.'

Herne looked across the saloon at him and nodded. He knew that Whitey had been right.

The batwing doors opened a little and Walt's bald, perspiring head poked through.

'Jesus Christ!' he whispered hoarsely. 'You killed all six of 'em!'

Coburn turned on him, anger clear in his voice. 'What in damnation did you expect? What did they think was going to happen? This weren't bottles on any damned wall!'

The barkeep looked with horror at his shattered mirror, then walked to the cripple kid's body. Several other townsfolk edged their way warily into the saloon and stood close together just inside the doors.

None of them spoke. Terrified eyes stared, trembling fingers pointed. They had seen the bodies outside; witnessed the speed of the shooting, the speed of the dying.

Now there were two more, one of them that nice Batson kid with one good leg who had been so polite whenever he was in town for supplies for his pa.

A kid who had been drunk enough to be dangerous with a gun was now an object of pity.

Walt turned slowly round from kneeling over the body. 'One of these bullets was in the back,' he said, shaking his head in a mixture of disbelief and sorrow.

'Damned right it was!' retorted Herne.

'Why?' Walt fingered the cut alongside his head and looked at the man he had helped earlier, helped and admired. Now . . .

'Why,' interrupted Coburn, his pink eyes small and fierce,

'is because the dumb bastard had his back to me at the time. You got any other fool questions?'

'But he was a cripple. To shoot a cripple in the back – did you need . . . I mean, wasn't there any other way?'

'Not when he was about to do the very same thing to Jed. What other kind of death you reckon backshooters deserve, Even those as bad at it as he was?'

Walt shook his head and walked between Herne and Coburn to the bar. Herne went and stood near him, reloading his Colt as he did so.

'It's like I said before, the ones you don't know about, the ones that ain't any real good – they're the ones you don't take risks with. Not if you want to go on living.'

The barkeep said nothing, just stared at the broken mirror and at his own shattered reflection. Neither told him anything.

Through the cracks in the mirror he watched Herne and Coburn quit the saloon.

The moon was fully covered now and the night was dark. The four bodies had been dragged or lifted away. Only the marks where they had fallen remained. That and the darkening stains of their blood upon the dust and dirt of the street.

Next morning when Herne and Coburn rose early and fetched their mounts from the livery stable, the bewhiskered old timer accepted their money without a word or a look. As soon as their backs were turned he spat into the straw.

The owner of the general store said nothing either; his hands shook as they accepted payment. The girl who served them with their breakfast had no smile for Jed Herne that morning.

Neither man minded; neither had expected anything different. It was ever the same. Friendliness, pride at their presence, always turned to coldness and hostility after a shoot-out like that one.

No one attempts to pat the head of a lion fresh from its kill, its jaws, its claws still redolent of the blood of its prey.

Herne and Coburn ate in silence, paid their dues, mounted up and rode south out of town. Folk on the boardwalk turned their heads away as the two men rode past.

## Chapter Four

The clouds from the previous night had disappeared. The sky was a bright, uncluttered blue. Sharp and clear the way mornings sometimes are in the fall.

Herne and Coburn rode at a steady trot along the track which led between the hills, neither speaking, each one's thoughts his own.

At the point where the trail reached its highest point, they reined in their mounts and looked out over the valley.

The descent was sharp, taking them into a wide plain which stretched almost to the horizon without disturbance. A river meandered its way through the centre of the valley, the banks broadening and narrowing with its bends and straights. Away to the left, a further line of hills rose slowly, turning in towards the plain and framing it at the horizon itself.

The furthermost peaks were already layered with snow.

A gradual slope to the right was thickly covered with trees, firs towering green and tall above other branches heavy with leaves that had turned and were ready to fall: golds, yellows, reds, browns.

Whitey Coburn lifted his sweat-stained stetson and dragged the arm of his wool coat across his forehead.

'Know what?'

'What?'

'Time was I'd have seen that over there and thought nothin' 'bout it. Now it looks to me like a goddamn miracle.'

Herne followed his friend's gaze, down on to the wooded slope.

'Uh-hum. Guess you're right at that. Sure is somethin'.'

Herne scratched at his neck, steadying the movements of the horse under him with his knees. The animal was impatient to be on its way.

'Growin' old, Jed, that's what it is. When you get to feel that all you want t' do is sit an' stare at goddamn trees, maybe it's time t'do just that.'

'Meanin' what?'

Coburn slapped at a drowsy fly resting on his mount's neck. 'Meanin' I've got me a powerful hankerin' to settle down. I'm too old for this sort of life. Want to enjoy a few good years with a place of my own – some place like this, maybe. Sky as blue as that one up there, water runnin' close; cabin I built with my own hands. A woman to share it with, even a couple of kids. A son. Damnation, I sure would like to get me a son.'

He stopped abruptly and looked at Herne's darkening face. 'You know what I mean, don't you, Jed. You . . .'

'What the hell we doin' sittin' here and ramblin' on like two old women? We got places to be an' men to meet. Let's move out of here.'

He slapped the end of his reins down on his horse's flank and pushed his thighs downwards. The animal moved off sharply and Herne rode quickly down towards the valley, leaving Whitey Coburn to follow.

The albino's thoughts were still of some place he could retire to. A good life, free from danger. A beautiful young woman with blue eyes and soft hands.

Jed Herne's mind turned on less pleasant things. Memories triggered off by Coburn's words beat against the inside of his brain like the wings of trapped birds. He knew what Whitey had been talking about, right enough. Knew too well.

For Herne had set his gun aside and settled down in just such a place, with just such a woman. Louise. So much younger than him in years, so much older in wisdom. They had run their small spread together and apart from the child that had been still-born everything had been fine.

Louise had got pregnant again and Herne had not known. She had been saving the news until she was certain, until she could give the man she loved the surprise she knew he wanted more than anything else in the world.

But before she could break the news, their whole lives were ripped asunder. Men, drunken men, savage in their lust, had tramped over the snow to the cabin where Louise was alone save for a neighbour woman.

When they left, they left her raped brutally, the life that had quickened inside her body harshly dead. Louise could not face the prospect of carrying on after that. Not even with Jed.

She had hanged herself in their barn.

Yes, Herne had settled down all right. And in the end all he had to show for it were two dead children and the memory of a beautiful young woman who had put on her best dress in which to take her own life.

He heard Whitey moving his horse up alongside him and spurred his own animal ahead again. Right now, the last thing he wanted to do was talk: even to a friend.

The deeper they rode into the valley, the further it seemed to recede. The white crested hills were now both behind and beyond them.

Whitey Coburn spat out the last remnants of his plug of chewing tobacco.

'Tell you somethin',' he called ahead to Herne's back.

Jed wheeled about and came alongside the albino. He had had enough of his own company. 'Tell away.'

'Seems we talked so little 'bout this job of yorn, I don't even know where in hell's name we're headed or what we got to do when we get there.'

Herne grunted. 'Right now we're due at a little place

called Davis, down east of the Brazos. Meet a couple of men. They're the ones who put out the contract.'

'What is it, Jed?' Despite what he had said before, Coburn's eyes showed his eager anticipation of excitement to come. 'Some gang to chase down? Gold shipments to protect? A town to clean up? What is it?'

'A mess of pots.'

'What?!'

Herne grinned, almost in spite of himself. 'Pots.'

'What kind of damned pots you talkin' about.'

'Antiquities, they called them.'

'Who?'

'The two we're riding to meet.'

Coburn looked up at the clear blue of the sky and blinked. 'Jesus! Sweet Jesus Christ! An' I was thinkin' that if I was goin' to go out then I'd do it with one real big one – so what do we get? Playin' nursemaid to a pile of junk!'

Herne's grin broadened and he reached over and slapped his friend on the arm. 'Don't worry, Whitey. You was the one said you was gettin' too old. Least the pots won't make too fast a run for it!'

Coburn reached inside his coat for a piece of tobacco and bit off a piece savagely. 'I tell you straight, Jed. It would have been different if I'd known what the cussed job was.'

Herne looked at him sharply. 'You mean you had other things you could have done?'

'Course.'

'Like hell you did! How far d'you ride to get to me?'

There was a long pause, then Whitey said quietly: 'Somewhere's around Denver.'

'You rode all the way from Colorado down through Cheyenne and Commanche territory and into Texas on account of you'd heard some rumour in a saloon that I was lookin' for men. You did that and there were other offers?'

Coburn chewed on without answering. Herne didn't push him further; he knew what it was like when you were a gunfighter with a reputation that had lived on and on. Most folk thought you were dead; the rest figured you already had one foot in Boot Hill.

He saw the expression on Coburn's face and reflected on his friend's yearnings for a life of settlement and peace. No matter how hard he stared he could see nothing of that in the albino's strange face. He thought he could read something else there, but turned his head away before he could be sure.

If it was what he had imagined, he didn't want to know.

'What the hell is it?' Whitey demanded.

'Nothin'. Why?'

'You looked as though you'd seen a ghost or somethin', that's what.'

'Nonsense, Whitey. That's plumb foolish an' you know it.'

But Coburn had been right – and the ghost Herne had glimpsed was all too familiar: the long white hair which fell around the skull, the two pink eyes that stared from the sockets of bone.

They were within sight of the small town of Davis when Coburn turned in his saddle and spoke with the tone of someone who has long had something nagging at his brain. 'Hell, I don't even know how much we're gettin' paid for this damned job!'

'Guess you don't.' Herne smiled wryly. 'Thought if'n you did you'd have maybe gone back the way you come. No matter how far.'

'Sweet Jesus, Jed! What do we reckon to get out of this?'

'Little less than a thousand.'

Coburn looked up at the sky, then spat off to the side. 'How much less?'

'We'll get eight hundred.'

'Each?'

'Between us.'

The animal under Coburn whinnied and stamped as the

rider's hand pulled in tight on the rein. 'Ain't no time to be jokin', Jed.'

'It ain't no joke. That's the pay they offered.'

'An you took that?'

'Didn't seem to have a whole lot of choice.'

'Shit!'

Whitey urged his horse into a fast trot, then a gallop. Jed let him get some way ahead before he set out after him. It wasn't long before the albino was looking back over his shoulder, a smile starting to cross his face.

'You realize I ain't never worked for less than that. Not even ten, twenty years back.'

'I know,' Herne shouted as he caught up with him.

'But like you said, there don't seem to be a whole lot of choice . . . Sure don't.'

Herne slowed to a walk and Coburn did the same. Then they stopped and looked at the line of buildings spread out below them. Almost everything was ranged along the one street; false-fronted buildings whose backs were a storey lower than their other side suggested. At the far end there was a scattering of squat dwellings that seemed to be made out of mud, baked hard in the Texas sun. Beyond the town, to the east, the wooden grave markers showed clearly on the hill.

For a small place there were a hell of a lot of graves.

'Whitey.'

'Yep?'

'This could take a long time.'

Coburn stared at his friend and the lines of age and hard living showed clear on his face like the work of wind on white rock. 'Don't matter none, Jed. I bin goin' nowhere for ten years.'

The two men they had come to meet were obvious as soon as Herne and Coburn entered the largest of Davis' two saloons. They stepped under the swaying sign that proclaimed *The*

*Brazos Queen* and pushed their way through the batwing doors.

It was an entrance that failed to go unnoticed. It wasn't intended to.

Drinkers paused with glasses midway to their lips, mouths hung open in mid-conversation. Even the faro dealer stopped with his hand in the air above the table.

The woman sitting on the edge of the bar slid down till her feet were on the floor, rucking her dress up behind her as she did so and giving anyone interested a good glimpse of white thigh above a purple garter and dark stockings.

No one was interested.

The two gunfighters stood their ground, waiting until all of the customers had had their fill of staring; until they had weighed them up for what they were and decided to leave well alone.

Only when the low hum of conversation had started up once more, and the clink of glasses could be heard, did Herne and Coburn walk into the centre of the saloon.

There was a raised section at the rear with wooden partitions dividing it into booths. Their contacts were sitting in one of these, different from everyone else on account of their clothes and the space that had been left around them.

As Herne and Coburn walked towards them, both men exchanged a hasty glance and downed the remains of whatever had been in their glasses.

Jed wondered what they had to be so nervous about.

'Gentlemen.'

'Mister Herne.'

'We were expecting you yesterday.'

Herne nodded. 'Took a mite longer than I reckoned. Findin' help weren't easy.'

'And this is what you found?' said the darker of the two, pointing a finger at Coburn.

Whitey's hand moved for his gun and Jed reached his own hand across and stopped him.

The man who had spoken first half stood up from his seat and smiled earnestly. 'Gentlemen. Gentlemen. There is no call for any animosity. None whatsoever. We both have complete confidence in Mister Herne's choice of companion in this – er – venture. Please sit down and relieve your undoubted thirst. Then when you are refreshed we may discuss business.'

The smile stayed on the man's face as if it were stuck there. Herne and Coburn sat down opposite each other and waited while more glasses and another bottle were called for.

The one who was doing most of the talking introduced himself as Floyd Toomey. A New Orleans lawyer, he had met Herne while on a visit to Dallas and had offered him the job there and then.

He was a large man, both tall and fat – probably the weight of the two gunfighters combined. His suit was dark with thin white and grey stripes running through it and Herne guessed it would have cost the best part of his own share of the pay for delivering the lawyer's damned pots safely. A rather grubby looking white shirt frilled out from underneath the jacket and a silver stick pin with some kind of stone at its head was thrust down into one lapel. His hair was slicked back and down with a quantity of grease and perfume that still smelled strongly even among the other pungent odours of the saloon.

The second man looked to be a half breed. Toomey introduced him as Antonio Thursby, an associate from New Orleans. His face was swarthy, with sharp features and two dark eyes that were never still. He, too, wore an expensive suit, a silver chain stretched across the black of his waistcoat, a soft pink handkerchief tumbling from the breast pocket of his coat.

When he drank, a gold tooth shone from the front of his mouth.

'You know the outline of what I require you to do, Mister Herne, that much remains the same.'

Herne looked across at Toomey and nodded, waiting for the big man to continue.

'Very well, yes – er – the shipment will be brought to a town called La Rosita. It is across the Rio Grande and on the edge of the Burro Mountains. By the river known as the Salado. There you will meet a man called Don Vincento. He will deliver to you a wagon containing the antiquities my associate and I desire. In exchange you will pay him a certain – er – sum of money.'

Toomey stopped abruptly, reaching for his glass and drinking hastily. Alongside Herne, the half-breed's eyes flickered more nervously than usual.

'This money,' Herne asked. 'How much is it?'

Toomey blinked, the action almost lost in the centre of his heavily bejowled face. 'Five thousand U.S. dollars, Mister Herne. Five thousand dollars.'

Coburn whistled through closed teeth.

'Course I don't know much about such things,' said Herne, 'But that sounds like a whole lot of money for a pile of pots and suchlike.'

Toomey fixed back on his smile and leaned forward across the table. His breath was sickly and sweet; his voice was low.

'Sir, I assure you these antiquities are most rare. Most rare. They will fetch a good price in the museums and private collections of our country. And not only here. There are many in Europe who would pay dearly to get their hands on such things.'

'How come no one else has?'

'That, Mister Herne, is our little business secret. But – er – shall we say that the authorities in those countries from where these pieces originate would not be pleased to know of their disappearance.'

The large head moved back across the table; the thick fingers sought out the glass once more. Thursby picked at his teeth with a silver toothpick he had slipped from his waistcoat pocket.

Herne looked at Coburn and said nothing. He didn't have a good feeling about what was going on. Not at all. From the expression of distrust on Whitey's face, neither did he. But there didn't seem to be anything specific to question.

'After La Rosita, then what?'

'As arranged, Mister Herne, you and your – er – colleague deliver the goods to New Orleans and collect the second half of your payment.'

Coburn's clenched fist hit the surface of the table hard. Thursby's eyes flashed and his right hand moved towards his coat pocket.

'Way I see it, if these damned things are worth so much, we ought to be gettin' more'n we are.'

Herne held his breath, aware of Thursby's movement, watching the half-breed's arm and Toomey's face at the same time.

Floyd Toomey shrugged his massive shoulders. 'I can – er – sympathize with your outburst, sir, but please remember that a business arrangement is, shall we say, sacred. Mister Herne and myself have made a deal and we shall, I'm sure, adhere to it strictly. You were doubtless aware of the financial details before you accepted your part in this – er – contract.'

Whitey's hand opened and closed, one, twice, three times.

Herne moved his tongue around his lips; they felt unnaturally dry. 'Could be my friend has a point. We didn't talk about how much money we was goin' to carry down into Mexico. If'n we had, then I might have asked more for doin' it.'

Thursby spoke for the first time, his voice thin and oddly accented. 'But you didn't. You didn't.' The dark eyes ceased moving and fixed themselves on Herne's face.

Toomey leaned forward. 'My associate is, of course, right. But at the same time I appreciate your feelings.' He stood up. 'Shall we say that – er – if you deliver the goods to New Orleans within a reasonable time and in perfect condition, then I shall be pleased to pay you a more than handsome bonus.'

Herne nodded. He stood and accepted Toomey's outstretched hand. The flesh was flabby, but the bone was firm underneath. He was not a man to underestimate, Herne decided, whatever appearances might suggest to the contrary. Nor was the dark man with him.

Whitey Coburn nodded and stepped away from the table, waiting for Jed to be done. He wanted another drink but he wanted it in some other place, some other company.

Herne joined him and they stepped down into the base of the saloon, men's eyes moving to follow them once more. Their easy, balanced step, the guns strapped and tied to their sides, the unwavering eyes that nevertheless saw everything: these were two men who would step aside for nothing, for no one.

Neither spoke till they were outside in the street.

'Guess I shouldn't have done that, Jed, seeing as how it's your show, but goddam, I couldn't hold myself back. Those two, they riled me just by sittin' there. That fat lawyer with his fine clothes an' his fancy way with words – reckon he'd get a knife slipped across your throat soon as look at you.'

'Know what you mean, Whitey. But they got the money an' we ain't. They're buyin' an' we're sellin'. That's how it is.'

'I know.'

They crossed the street and walked along past the saddler's and the gunsmith's towards the building which advertised itself as the Davis Rooming House. Except that the end of the board had started to fall away and the last three letters of House had fallen with it. Not that it worried Herne and Coburn none: as long as the beds were all of a piece that would be enough.

They wanted a good meal and a good night's rest before heading south west towards the Rio Grande and the Mexican border.

Herne paid for their room in advance, dipping into one of the two envelopes Floyd Toomey had handed to him at the end of their conversation. The other one held the five thousand dollars.

## Chapter Five

They decided to follow the Brazos south out of Davis, quitting it only when the last of the high land that swept down from the centre of Texas had been left behind. Their trail then led almost directly westwards, giving them the chance of taking in San Antonio or steering well clear.

Herne thought it best to swing round below the town, keeping to less well-used tracks and smaller settlements. If the route proved to be a good one, and wide enough to bring a wagon through, they would make use of it for the return journey.

The intention was to pick up the Nueces river and follow its winding course towards the Rio Grande. As the Mexicans knew it: the Rio Bravo del Norte. Past Crystal City, they would cross the Rio Grande at Eagle Pass.

La Rosita was less than a hundred miles from there, always with the heavy peaks of the Serrenias del Burro towering northwards as they rode.

The two men had packed ample supplies, although they expected to replenish them on the way. Hard tack, bacon, beans, coffee, a generous amount of tobacco for Coburn, and a deal of ammunition.

Herne was carrying his well-worn single shot .55 Sharps in the bucket holster which ran underneath the flap of his saddle. Coburn preferred a Winchester .44-40, accurate over two hundred yards and with an extra sight at the top of the stock. Although it lacked the range and precision of Herne's rifle it did have speed of shot.

Between them, the guns made an efficient pair.

For four days the only time they were used was when Coburn shot them a couple of rabbits. The five thousand dollars rested safe underneath the thick wool of Jed's coat and there wasn't anybody around who looked interested in taking it away from him.

Which was the way both men liked it.

'Hey, Jed,' said Whitey towards the evening of that fourth day's ride, 'that girl – the one you was lookin' after on account of what happened to her ma along of your Louise – what happened to her, anyways?'

'School.'

'Uh-huh. She got relations send her?'

Herne shifted in the saddle and looked about them. Nothing but a flat landscape without a tree or a bush to break its monotony. Around the horizon the failing sun spread itself like a ring of weak gold.

He wasn't sure why he didn't like talking about Becky, but he seemed to get knotted inside whenever he did. Knotted in his head and in his stomach. He guessed maybe it was on account of her being the nearest thing to kin he had left in the world.

Unless you included Whitey.

'Jed? You hear me?'

'Sure I heard you. No one paid for her but me. Sent her over to England on the boat for a spell. She was draggin' me down and there were things to do.'

'Damn, Jed! That must have cost one hell of a lot of dollars.'

'Most of what I got from our spread an' stock.'

'That's why you went back to sellin' your gun after those years you was with Louise?'

'Maybe. Reckon I'd've done that anyway. Man makes one

attempt to change his life. That don't work out an' you go back to what you know best. What you're born to.'

It was Coburn's turn to be silent ... his own attempt at settling down was yet to come. And he felt a yearning for it, a longing for the peace it would bring. Smooth white hands holding sparkling, yellow gold.

When the line at the land's edge had lessened to a single strand of weak white light, Coburn spoke again. 'Jed, 'stead of camping out here tonight, how about you an' me finding somewheres to get ourselves good and rollin' drunk?'

Jed smiled. Normally he wouldn't have been taken with the idea. But things had been kind of dull of late. Besides, Whitey wasn't the only one with ideas going on inside him that a couple of bottles would set to sleep.

'Why not?' he replied. 'If'n we hurry along we should reach a cantina before it's too late.

It was a border town like any other. So anonymous it didn't even seem to have a name. Fifteen or so buildings huddled together, some made out of planks roughly hewn and nailed, others out of baked mud and clay. A couple of hundred yards away from these buildings there was a scattering of tents, showing clearly despite the darkness.

The cantina wasn't named either, but the noise and the light that spilled out showed the two men where it was. No door, just a space with a low arch framing it.

They stepped through.

There were half a dozen men sitting in a circle to the right of the room. One of them held a cockerel by its neck and wing, restraining it from movement while he discussed its virtues. They all seemed to be Mexican, swarthy skinned and wearing light coloured peasant clothes, their hair tied at the back or pushed under wide brimmed sombreros.

They turned slowly as the Americans came in, their conversation dying out and their dark eyes running over the newcomers. The cock freed its wing and flapped loudly and wildly in its owner's grasp.

Herne walked over to the heavy wooden table on the other side of the room which was serving as a bar. Two women in brightly embroidered blouses and slit black skirts moved aside to let him through. An old man sitting behind the table raised his head and stared up at Herne, his eyes unwavering.

'Senor?'

'Can you fix us something to eat?'

The man spoke quickly to the older of the two women, so that Herne was only able to pick out the occasional word. But it must have been all right.

'Si, senor. Tortillas.'

'That's fine.'

'Tequilla, senor?'

The old man was already reaching under the table for a bottle when Herne answered. The glasses were dirty, fingerprints clear on the grease and dust. The Mexican saw the expression on Herne's face and wiped the glasses quickly with a piece of cloth he picked up from the table. It left them dirtier than before.

'How about a place to sleep?'

'Senor?'

'Sleep.'

The man shrugged. 'There is a room at the back. You can sleep there. But . . .'

'But what?'

The man smiled. 'There are no beds.'

'We'll use our bed rolls.'

Herne took hold of the bottle by the neck and Coburn stretched down for the glasses. As they were moving away, the old Mexican called Herne back.

He shifted his glance immediately to the woman still sitting by the table. 'Yvitta – she has room with bed.'

Herne looked at her. Dark hair hung in curling waves

about an oddly sallow face. Her lips were painted bright crimson and her cheeks rouged and powdered in almost exact circles. Herne could see the steady rise and fall of her breasts underneath the thin material of her white blouse, the large nipples pressing on the cotton. The long fingers of her right hand moved slowly along her thigh, below the point where the skirt split.

'Thanks,' said Herne. 'We'll take the room out back.'

He turned quickly but not before the girl had pouted angrily at him and flashed her eyes dangerously. However little Mexican Herne understood, it was clear that she knew English well enough.

Back at the stained round table, Whitey Coburn was not looking any happier.

'What's up?'

'Those bastards over there keep turnin' round and starin' at me. Then back again and laughin' to each other. I ain't about to stand for that.'

Herne poured his friend a full glass of tequilla and a half glass for himself. If it tasted as rough as he thought it would, he wasn't about to take too many chances.

The Mexicans continued to swivel their heads and laugh. No matter what Herne could say to the contrary, it was obvious that the object of their amusement was Coburn with his strange albino appearance.

Jed could sense his friend getting increasingly tense, closer and closer to the point where he must burst over into violent action. Yet he did not want to risk a fight here and now. Another day would see them close to La Rosita.

'Damn those bastards!' said Coburn, swallowing back a shot of tequilla and coughing as the rawness tore at the back of his throat.

'Take it easy, Whitey. They bin drinkin', that's all. They're more interested in that prize fighting cock of their's than they are in you.'

As he said that, three of them laughed aloud once again.

Once too often.

Coburn stood up fast, pushing table, bottle and glasses to the floor. His Colt was in his hand and anger burnt fiercely in his pink eyes. Lines of fury were etched strongly on his face.

'Right! Now which of you Mex bastards thinks I'm so all-fired funny? Let's see you laugh now.'

Silence. Only the cockerel still flapping its wings and trying to turn its head from side to side. Dark, wide eyes stared upwards at the strange, white-haired Americano with the palest of faces.

Coburn stepped forward, kicking the table sideways towards the girl beside the bar. The other woman appeared with plates of food in her hands and stopped in her tracks, a steady drip of sauce falling from one of the sloping plates.

'Come on, you cowardly drunken shitkickers! Laugh! Laugh, damn it!'

Herne watched the old man for any signs of movement but there were none. The group of Mexicans still hadn't made any effort to say or do a thing. It was doubtful if any of them were carrying guns, although one or two would certainly have knives. But faced with Coburn's Colt and his obvious temper they were not about to do anything foolish.

Suddenly all of them were very sober.

'Well? What happened to the joke?'

Some of them started to back away as he advanced upon them. They flinched as Coburn's left hand reached down and seized the bottle from in front of them and swung it back by the neck, pouring the contents down his throat.

He held the bottle high and flung it against the far wall, where it smashed and bounced back into the cantina in fragments.

'See that, you bastards? Was that pretty funny, too?'

The cockerel freed itself from its owner's grip at last and threw back its head in a loud crow of triumph, wings at full stretch, red and brown, striped with black.

Coburn fired fast and the sound of the cockerel was lost in the roar of the gun: it was not to start again. The head had been blown into nothingness. Everyone stared as the headless bird ran round in a frantic circle, blood spouting wildly from its severed neck.

Whitey took another pace forward and kicked out with his boot, sending the dying cock into the middle of the terrified Mexicans.

They jumped back and shouted out with a mixture of fright and anger. Seconds later all of them had run through the archway and out into the night.

Coburn turned round to look at Herne; the anger was still evident in his eyes. He pushed the Colt down into his holster and bent down to pick up the table.

Herne said nothing, just got up and went over to the old man for another bottle of tequilla. As he stood there the girl with the rouged cheeks rested the back of her hand against the outside of his leg. Jed noticed, but did nothing to move it until he walked back to where the plates of tortillas were waiting.

Coburn greeted him with a grin.

'You feelin' a lot better for that?' Herne asked.

'Damned right! Tell you what, though.'

'What's that?'

'I'm plumb glad we ain't about to eat no chicken!'

Herne bit into the spicey food and washed it down with more of the strong liquor. The girl who had stroked his thigh was becoming more attractive by the minute, more desirable. He was aware of a stirring in his groin; a longing that he had not been able to satisfy properly for too many empty nights.

Whitey noticed his friend's interest and chuckled into his glass. 'Seems to me you're goin t' get a better bed than you bargained for.'

'I don't know . . .'

'Then you're a fool, Jed. An' that's one thing I didn't

reckon you to be. Ain't nothin' wrong with takin' a little creature comfort on the trail. Sides, she ain't a bad lookin' woman.'

'How about you?'

Coburn refilled his glass and dug his fork down into the tortilla. 'All I want to do is sit here and finish this bottle. After that, I'll stretch out in back and get me a good sleep. You I'll see in the mornin'.'

Herne nodded and bolted down the remains of his food. The girl was staring at him openly, her nipples dark against the white material and her legs parted in more than a promise.

He stood up, nodded to Whitey, then stepped over to the girl. A few moments later they walked out of the cantina together, leaving Coburn alone with an old Mexican and the body of a mutilated cockerel.

It didn't seem to bother him none: not at all.

The stars showed clear through the open window of the girl's room. Yvitta. She had said her own name again and again. Yvitta make you happy. Yvitta make it good for you. Yes, now, you do ... ooh, yes that is good. Yvitta will ...

The straw was caught in clusters under the cover of the mattress and where some of it stuck through it scraped roughly against Herne's back as he moved from side to side, up and down. The Mexican girl straddled him, her smooth brown thighs alongside his chest as she rocked above him, drawing his strength deeply inside her. One hand pressed down upon Herne's chest, the warm palm circling faster and faster, while the fingers of the other squeezed the nipples of her own breasts.

Herne closed his eyes and tried to concentrate on what was taking place; on the warm wetness that enclosed him and slid around him; on the sound of the girl's voice ... She moved her hand to his mouth and he bit down into the soft flesh at its side, gently at first then harder, harder ...

Whitey Coburn was still sitting at the same table when they came in. The woman had reappeared and taken away his plate; the second bottle was close to being finished. He was about ready to turn in.

They burst through the open door of the cantina and this time they had guns. Nor were they the same frightened peasants as before. Coburn recognized the one who had owned the fighting cock, perhaps one other. The rest were older, more determined. Ammunition belts crossed their chests in the manner of Mexican banditos.

Their leader had a straggly moustache and a scar that showed clearly through the dark skin and stubble of beard as it traced its way jaggedly down the length of his face. He also had a pistol – and it was already drawn and cocked.

There were five others: three had guns drawn. Two didn't. Yet.

Coburn blinked and cursed inwardly. Not that there was any sense in doing that. Not now. What he had to do was get out alive. And by himself.

The leading Mexican looked Coburn up and down, then sneered. 'When they told me of the gringo with white hair and pink eyes I did not believe them. I thought that they had been drinking too heavily. But now . . .' He gestured with the barrel of his gun. '. . . now I can see with my own eyes they were telling me the truth. A gringo who is like a rat, a white rat with little pink eyes. A rat who is only good for shooting at cockerels!'

Whitey threw the bottle that was close to his left hand and fell fast to his right. He heard the roar of the Mexican's gun, loud in the confined space of the cantina. He rolled and pushed himself up into a crouch, banging against another table as he did so. His Colt was drawn and clear and the first shot smacked into the centre of the Mex's crotch. There was a scream of pain and two more shots, one upon the other. The one that was Coburn's took another of the Mexicans high in the chest and sent him staggering back against the white wall, blood pumping through his shirt and staining his gun belt.

Whitey jumped over the bar table, pushing the old man to the floor. He turned the table over and ducked down behind it. As he did so a shot thudded into the end of it and another one raked along the wall behind him.

He took a quick glance over the edge. Two had jumped back outside the cantina and were trying to take snap shots round the open doorway. One was lying flat, sheltering behind a couple of small tables and some chairs. A fourth stood in the middle of the room; his pistol was in his hand and it was pointing in Coburn's direction but the look of fear on his face made it doubtful that he would actually pull the trigger.

Coburn recognized him as the owner of the cockerel. He shot him in the face, changing the expression of terror into a mashed and bloody blur. To Whitey there seemed to be some kind of poetic justice about that.

There was a sudden volley from the door and he ducked low again, moving to the end of the table and transferring his Colt to his left hand. They had both followed through into the room and fired again. Whitey squeezed his trigger and got the first of them in the shoulder. He cursed and cut back along the floor.

The old man was stretched out with one arm raised up along the white wall. His mouth was open and a line of pale blood trickled over his cheek and on to his scrawny neck. There were two bullet wounds in his chest and another low in his belly.

At least they'd hit something.

Coburn stayed low and jammed fresh shells into the chambers of his Colt. In that moment of stillness he could hear the whimpering noises of the Mexican he had shot in the crotch.

Coburn smiled and peered over the top of the table. Beyond the wounded man, behind the Mex who had taken his in the face, something wriggled at floor level.

Coburn took a quick shot and grinned as a yelp told him he had hit something. Something that now sprang upwards in a final gesture of bravery and recklessness. He got as far as four feet away from Coburn before a bullet turned him full circle and dropped him across his two friends. The whimpering continued . . .

. . . Herne arched his back as mutual orgasm shook their bodies in a strained frenzy of climax. Eyes clenched tight shut he could not escape the vision that lowered its head towards him, eyes shining, mouth slightly open, smiling. Louise. His Louise. His wife. He shook his head and pushed upwards on the mattress. The face was still there, pink tongue teasing between full, warm lips. A spasm coursed through him: not Louise any more. Becky.

It was Becky's face closing on his: her body he imagined emptying himself into.

Herne flung a hand upwards and as he did so the first shots rang out from down the street.

His eyes opened fast. All they saw was the Mexican girl, Yvitta.

'Move!'

'Senor!'

'Get your arse off there!'

She lifted her right leg and Herne ducked out underneath, grunting as he did so. Hands reached for pants and gun. He was still pulling at his shirt as he ran out into the street.

He saw two Mexicans standing by the open door to the cantina, guns drawn. He didn't need to guess what was happening.

One of the men whirled round at the sound of Herne's approach, mouth open to shout out a question. Before the first word had had time to form itself on the man's lips, Herne shot him through the throat.

The second Mexican hesitated, knowing that he was caught between two fires. By the time he had decided to run,

Coburn had appeared in the doorway. He did not get far. A bullet drove him into a wall on the other side of the street and he pushed himself up on to his knees, hands raised in appeal, possibly in prayer.

Whitey Coburn steadied his arm and gave him due deliverance.

'Have a good time?' he asked Herne, as Jed came to a halt alongside him, looking into the interior of the cantina.

'Nothin' on what you had,' Herne replied stepping inside.

Coburn laughed and holstered his gun. In the corner the Mexican women was kneeling over the old man, lips moving fast, saying a litany of words without apparent meaning, beads passing through her fingers as tears fell on to the body of the dead man stretched out beneath her.

Coburn stepped into the middle of the room and yanked the wounded Mexican leader to his feet. The centre of his body was deep red and the insides of his legs ran with steady streams of blood.

'So I'm a white rat with pink eyes only good for shooting cocks, is that right?' hissed the albino.

Through his pain, the Mexican stared at Coburn in bewilderment. What was he going to do now, this strange gringo? Perhaps he would kill him. That would end the pain. Please God, let the gringo finish him off!

Coburn brought back his boot and kicked the man full force in the groin. The Mex stumbled backwards, a scream spluttering from between his lips. Coburn wiped the toe of his boot on the dead body of the one he had shot through the head and turned to face Herne.

'If you've all finished here, I guess I have. Stayin' the night don't seem such a good idea after all.'

It didn't at that.

The two men walked out of the cantina, leaving it to the prayers of a terrified woman and the agonies of a slowly dying man.

## Chapter Six

It was a misty fall morning. The lower slopes of the Serrenias del Burro were swathed in curves of slow moving mist. The higher peaks beyond could only be imagined.

Jed Herne pulled off his scarred leather gloves and blew warm air into the cupped palms of his hands. It had to be ten degrees colder than the day before. Damn it!

He lifted one hand and pushed the fingers through his greying hair, breaking the tangled knots that had formed. Directly to the south he saw the dust of a rider moving fast towards him. He put his left-hand glove back on; eased the Colt from its holster with his right and spun the chambers, enjoying the beautifully oiled movement, the purring sound.

Herne walked briskly to his left, heading for the rise where his horse was tethered. The clouds of dust were nearer, the shape of the man bending over the saddle as yet indistinct.

Herne reached over his saddle and gripped the stock of his Sharps. He pulled it clear and seconds later the shiney, worn wood was against his cheek as he squinted along the sights.

Moments passed: Jed lowered the rifle: reversed it and slid it back into its place. It was Whitey Coburn.

The lean albino slowed as he came closer, hand stroking his animal's neck and mane, steadying it now. He rode directly to where Herne was waiting and lifted his right leg from the stirrup, jumping to the ground before the horse had come to a standstill.

'What in hell's name's after you?'

Coburn grinned: 'Not a damned thing!'

'You mean you got fed up with that mount of yorn an' you're drivin' her into the ground for the sake of it.'

'No. Just felt like lettin' her have her head, that's all.'

'Okay. What'd you find out?'

Coburn drew breath heavily and squatted down on his haunches; for a moment he let his head flop forward, white hair tumbling around it. 'Tell you, I didn't like the feelin'. Not one little bit. Small town but she's full to overflowin' with folk. Too many Mexes walkin' round with guns all over 'em and mean looks on their faces.'

'Hell,' Herne interrupted, 'it is Mexico. What d'you expect to find?'

Coburn looked up at him. 'I know that, Jed. But there were just too many of 'em. Like they was waitin' to start their own damned revolution or somethin'. We get ourselves in trouble in that place an' more 'n' a hundred guns goin' t' blast us from there to eternity.'

Herne nodded. His friend had been around enough to be able to sense out trouble when it was in the offing. And since the men he was supposed to be meeting were waiting for him in the middle of that same trouble, that made things more than complicated.

Whitey was right, though. No sense in riding in with a sizeable sum of money in U.S. dollars – especially when folk knew that was what you would be toting.

'What d'you reckon, Jed?'

'Reckon we'll have to get them to ride out of town and meet us. That way we'll be more likely to control what goes down.'

'How we goin' t' do that?'

Herne pointed past the trail Coburn had taken back from La Rosita. 'There's a road goes in along of the Salado. We'll send us in a message, arrange a meeting with them. They can come to us, drive the wagon out towards the higher ground where the river forks to the north east.'

'Suppose they won't? Suppose they don't believe the message?'

Herne shrugged: 'If'n that happens we'll think again. But I don't see no reason why they shouldn't ride out – not if they want that money bad enough. It's not as if they got a whole lot to lose.'

Coburn stood up and stepped across to his horse, loosening its girth and preparing to pull the saddle free and rub the sweat from its body.

'I sure ain't got no better idea,' he said. 'An' anything keeps me from shootin' my way out of that town suits me fine.' The weathered face shifted into a wry smile. 'Damned if I didn't kill me enough Mexes for one week.'

He turned away from Herne and Jed watched the narrow, powerful back as it leaned slightly forward over his horse. For some reason he could neither pin down nor begin to understand with any clarity, it was suddenly as if he was looking at a man he no longer knew, as though the person in front of him were a stranger.

Late afternoon. Even the lower parts of the mountain range were obscured. Herne and Coburn sat on either side of a small fire, watching the flames lick round the bottom of the enamel coffee pot. Whitey was chewing his tobacco and turning his head to one side every now and then so as to squirt a stream of brown liquid on to the ground.

Herne leaned forward and lifted the pot from the fire with his gloved hand. He poured the dark coffee into two battered tin mugs and passed one across to Coburn. The steam rose from the surfaces of the coffee and became mingled with their breath.

'Sit round here much longer an' we'll be froze to death. That or it'll be too dark t' see anyone comin'.'

'Maybe that's what they're bankin' on.'

'Could be. We gonna sit here and find out?'

Jed drank from the mug and flinched as the hot coffee

burnt the back of his throat. 'We're goin' t' find out right enough, only we ain't goin' t' be sittin' here doin' it. Soon as we done finished this, we'll shift back up into them trees an' wait there.'

Coburn nodded and sipped at his drink. 'Uh-huh. An' if no one comes at all?'

'Let's worry 'bout that later.'

When they were ready, they moved upwards on the slope, leaving the last of the fire to burn. Their horses were still tied close by and there were enough of their things down by the fire to draw in anybody interested.

They had only been in the shadow of the trees for fifteen minutes when they heard hoofbeats.

'One.' said Herne quietly.

Coburn nodded and edged away to the left, drawing his gun from its holster as he moved. Herne rested his right hand on the butt of his Colt and stayed where he was, eyes peering down into the steadily darkening distance.

The rider materialized, coming slow and careful; a rifle was already in his hand, resting at an angle across the saddle pommel. He wore a wide-brimmed hat, the edges of which curled upwards and round. From one side a tall black feather stuck up above the top of the hat and was silhouetted against the background.

He reined in his mount thirty yards from the fire. Waited. From their hiding place, Herne and Coburn waited also. Moments later the man began to step softly forwards, trying to make as little noise as possible with his boots on the rough ground.

Quiet as he was it was easy to pick out the sound of pistols being cocked. First one, then another. Triple clicks from the direction of the trees. Too well spaced apart for comfort.

The Mexican hesitated. Knew that his horse was too far away, the trees too far also. Realized that the rifle in his hands would be no good without a target to aim at ... whereas the fire was close enough to illuminate himself.

He raised the rifle slowly, holding it sideways towards the darkness of the trees, fingers well away from the trigger. Then he let it fall to the ground. It landed butt first, bounced once and was still.

Two shapes stepped from that dark simultaneously.

'Don Vincento?'

The Mexican shook his head.

One of the Colts jerked at him, asking more.

'I come from him.' The voice was steady, its owner unafraid.

Herne came down towards the fire, showing his face. Coburn moved round in a curve, watching the Mexican from the rear at the same time keeping an eye on the trail he had used. He might have friends close by.

'You are Herne?'

'Yes.'

'That is good. Don Vincento sent me to you. He wishes to meet you.'

'That's fine. I sent for him to come here.'

The Mexican allowed a smile to appear at the edges of his wide mouth. 'Si, Senor Herne. Si. But Don Vincento is a careful man. Just as you are yourself.'

He glanced hastily over his shoulder to check the whereabouts of Herne's companion.

'So what does he say, your Don Vincento?'

'Tomorrow an hour before the middle of the day. Five miles south of La Rosita. Take the road beyond the town. There is a place where the river swings to the east. The land is flat. There are no hills and ...' He looked behind Herne meaningfully. '... no trees. Don Vincento will be there with the goods you are to purchase. He says to remind you to bring the money with you when you ride. You and your amigo.'

Herne nodded and put up his gun; he stepped swiftly forward and picked up the rifle from the ground, handing it back to the Mexican.

'Tell him we will be there.'

'Si, Senor. I will do this.'

The Mexican turned and walked back to his horse, trying not to stare at the other American's white hair showing clearly in the dusk. That, too, would be something to tell Don Vincento. There had been rumours of such a man, fast and deadly with a gun. A man without feeling, without compassion.

And now he had met Herne, also. The one they called Herne the Hunter above the Rio Bravo del Norte.

Only two, but such a pair!

He smiled once more as he pulled himself up into the saddle. Don Vincento would think of a way. He always did.

What Don Vincento did decide on was a fine welcome. Not one but two wagons. A strong fire with a spit erected over it on which a side of beef was turning and roasting. Round the sides of this, heavy black pots bubbling with deep red chilli beans. A long rough-wood table and chairs.

And eight armed men.

Yes, it was a fine welcome.

Herne and Coburn exchanged glances as they made their way towards the camp, set close to the steadily flowing river. They noted the rifles, the pistols, even a couple of sabres doubtless taken from the Mexican army.

The two men dismounted and allowed strange hands to lead their horses away to the line where the other mounts were tethered. One of the Mexicans got up from a chair at the centre of the table and extended both hands in their direction.

'Amigos! Is good to see you!'

He strutted round the table towards them, head held backwards at an angle so that his pointed beard jutted out before him like the prow of a ship. His stomach protruded from underneath the cross of his ammunition belts, resting on the thick leather of a third belt at the top of his pants.

Coburn was reminded of the fighting cock he had shot the head off in the cantina.

'Senor Herne! You and your friend are welcome.' He swept one arm behind him. 'You will eat with us, no?'

Herne shrugged. 'How 'bout our business?'

'Ah, senor, first let us celebrate our friendship. We have a saying, the man who eats meat with another will not spill his blood. Come!'

He walked back to the table and Herne and Coburn had little alternative but to follow. Besides, the smell of the food was making the juices of their hunger flow.

They sat opposite Don Vincento and watched as he shouted to his men and gestured towards the river. Two of them hauled in a rope that was fixed around the top of a thick pole. The surface of the water broke and a crate of wine rose up, splashing and glistening.

'Even in this weather, the wine she is good cold.'

He smiled and showed four gaps in the top of his teeth, several of the others black with decay. A hand stretched sideways and a bottle was placed in it, already opened. He set the neck to his mouth and swallowed hastily, then belched loudly.

'Is good to taste before offering to one's guests, yes?'

He poured wine lazily into the glasses in front of Herne and Coburn, his hand seemingly unsteady, the dark red liquid running on to the already stained table. He called two of his men and told them to sit down, pouring wine for them, then shouting for another bottle.

'This is Diego, this José. They are my – your expression I think is right hand men, no?'

Herne nodded and drank some of the wine. It was rough, strong, biting at the back of the throat, the roof of the mouth. Instantly, Don Vincento leaned forward and refilled his glass.

The Mexican's eyes shifted to Coburn. 'He is your right hand also, yes?'

'Sure is. Isaiah Coburn.'

'Senor Coburn, I think we have heard a little of your exploits. Even here in Mexico.'

He offered Coburn his hand but the albino ignored it, staring at it as though it were contaminated. Herne sensed the tension mount around the table. Diego and José both sat further back, freeing their gun hands so that they were ready for action.

Herne drew the Mexican leader's attention. 'Don Vincento, you have the goods with you? The ones we have come to buy?'

Don Vincento pointed towards the wagons, splashing the wine from his glass as he did so. 'Si, Senor Herne, all is there in crates and ready for you to take across the border. You have the money?'

Herne patted his coat with his left hand. 'It's here, right enough. All five thousand dollars of it.'

The Mexican's hand opened and the glass fell to the table and smashed. His mouth clamped tight shut, the dark eyes narrowing in his round face.

His companions at the table let their glasses alone, turning inwards to face the two Americans. Coburn and Herne allowed their hands to shift to the edge of the table, close to their guns.

Around them, the other Mexicans appeared to be carrying on with the preparations for the meal.

'Five thousand dollars.'

The words came from between the gaps in the man's teeth, hissed out like the venom of a snake that finds itself betrayed.

'Five thousand.'

Herne stared back at him. 'That's what I said.'

'Then there is no deal.'

'That was what we were given. The amount we was told.'

The Mexican's tongue showed between his lips, rounded and pink; the pupils of his eyes were still, like small, hard stones. 'The arrangement, she was for twice that. Ten thousand of your American dollars.'

Herne whistled softly and glanced at Coburn. The albino was sitting quite still, silently assessing their chances in the event of a sudden flare up.

Herne reached inside his coat, making the action slow and deliberate, not wanting to trigger off something that might yet be avoided. He pulled clear the envelope he had been given by Floyd Toomey and dropped it on the table between himself and Don Vincento.

'Take a look.'

A corner of the envelope began to darken as a pool of wine on the tables soaked through it. Don Vincento looked down and grabbed at it tearing the flap open. His hands greedily counted the crisp new notes. He looked quickly at Herne, then pushed the bills back inside the envelope and threw it back down on the table.

'Where are the rest?'

Herne tensed: 'There ain't no rest.'

'We were prom . . .'

Herne's fist thumped down on the table. 'That was how it was given to me. I ain't touched that damned envelope since Toomey give it me. He said you'd agreed on that price. That was between you an' him. My job was to see the money exchanged for those damned pots an' take 'em back. And that's what I aim to do.'

His voice was loud and clear. Everyone was looking at him now. The only movement that of the river on its way from the high mountains to the north.

Don Vincento pushed his hands down on the table and stood up, his stomach pulled in tight, anger evident in his stance. He moved his left hand nearer to one of the pair of pistols he wore at his side.

And then he belched.

And then he smiled.

He clapped both hands across his stomach and broke into

a harsh, grating laugh. 'So, that is the way it is senor. The way of business. We thought for ten thousand of your dollars. That would have made us very happy, would have bought many arms. Your employer has cheated us; he has cheated you also.' Don Vincento's head moved to one side and he roared with laughter again. His head leaned forward over the table. 'I tell you something, Senor Herne, these goods you take back to New Orleans. They are worth maybe five hundred dollars. Nothing.' He clapped his hands. 'You bring me five thousand dollars. So. Is not as much as I would like. But . . . is still good, no?'

He clapped his hands again and called for more wine. 'You will drink with me. Both of you. Put this money back in your coat until we have eaten. Then we shall make our exchange. We shall enjoy the meat together, yes? We shall be friends. Don Vincento and his Americano guests.'

Herne and Coburn drank from their glasses and then Herne took up the money and pushed it back inside his coat.

'You spoke of buying arms,' he said to Don Vincento. 'My friend said there were many men in town, many guns. There is a reason for all this?'

The Mexican nodded. 'Our country is torn. We have a President, Lerdo de Tejada. To the south of Mexico he is a good man. There the people thrive. But . . . here in the north everything is poverty. Lerdo wants us to live in a wasteland. And why?' He paused and looked at Herne and Coburn. Neither spoke.

'I will tell you why. Because he is frightened of you Americanos. He wants a wilderness between himself and attack from above the border. That wilderness, she is our land.'

The eyes were narrowing once more; the voice becoming tighter, more dangerous.

'General Porfirio Diaz, he will lead us to the share of the power that should be ours. We will bring riches to the north with our own blood.'

He swept the shattered glass from the table with his arm

and raised a wine bottle to his mouth and drank deeply.

'Come! Let us eat!'

The Mexican who wielded the knife had only one eye: where the right one had been there was now a vivid scar, wrinkled across its centre where the skin had knitted untidily together. This did not prevent him from slicing the meat with precision. The charred outside sent a strong smell up to the nostrils; the man's mouth visibly watered as he carved. Popping slices on to the tin plates that his colleague held ready.

Don Vincento had taken his own large portion first and passed on to receive a ladlefull of steaming beans from another of his followers.

Now it was Herne's turn.

The meat fell across the plate, its ends overlapping the edges. Three, four, five thick slices. The one-eyed man looked up at the American questioningly.

Herne shook his head: 'Uh-huh. That's fine.'

He passed on towards the pot of chilli beans. The man ladled on two portions which spread over the meat, filling in the spaces around it.

The man called Diego stepped across in front of Herne, coffee pot in one hand, empty mug in the other.

'You want coffee as well, senor?'

'Sure.' He stood, plate piled high with food in his left hand, and watched as the Mexican poured the coffee into the tin mug he now held in his right. Diego stopped when the liquid was less than half an inch from the top then stepped smartly aside.

Don Vincento was facing Herne. He no longer had food or drink in either hand: just his two guns.

'Now, Senor Herne, we shall take your five thousand dollars. After we have killed you . . .'

## Chapter Seven

A second stolen from time.

Jed Herne stood, palms upraised and weighted down; the Mexican less than ten feet away, both guns aiming directly at his chest.

The point of Don Vincento's beard thrust proudly forward, the swarthy features widened into a sneering laugh; the fingers tightened.

There was the sudden roar of a Colt .45 from close behind Herne.

The sound boomed in his ears and simultaneously the sneer on the Mexican's face disintegrated into a gory blur.

Herne dropped the plate and mug and pulled his own gun clear just as Coburn fired his second shot. What was remaining of Don Vincento's face exploded in a mass of splintered bone and gristle. Blood splashed out as the body staggered haphazardly. A solid spray of grey matter strongly flecked with crimson burst through the rear of the torn skull and fell on to one of the unused tin plates, slopping over the edge towards the ground.

Herne fired to his left. Diego had started to run for the cover of the nearest of the wagons as soon as the shooting had started. There had not been time for him to get far. The shell struck him low in his left side, inches above the hip. Somehow he managed to keep on running, one hand clutching his wound, his body bent low.

Herne dropped to one knee and levelled his gun. Coburn

squatted alongside him, sending two shots in the direction of a pair of Mexicans who were trying to get to the line of horses. They scuttled back behind cover, one hit in the leg and screaming with pain.

Diego never made it to the wagon. Herne's bullet took the crouching figure directly between the buttocks. The man jerked upright, both hands clasped in front of him where his genitals had been seconds before.

He fell forward and his head bounced up from the hard ground. Once only. His scream of agony died with him.

'That leaves six of the bastards, don't it?'

'Reckon.'

A shot rang out from the side of the furthest wagon, which was pulled round sideways towards the fire. It thumped into the side of beef so that it swung round on the spit.

'Ain't no use firin' at that, you dumb bastard!' yelled Coburn.

The gun poked into sight again and Whitey steadied his right arm with his left. He calmly squeezed the trigger and nodded with satisfaction as the arm was pulled hastily back, letting the weapon fall to the floor.

Two shots ran into the earth too close to Herne for comfort.

'Let's get the hell away from this fire!'

Coburn didn't answer: he had already started to run.

The albino made off in a zig-zag pattern, heading towards the second wagon, firing sporadically as he went. Herne let him have a couple of covering shots, then jumped to his right and scooped up one of Don Vincento's pistols.

He ran directly at the nearest wagon, emptying his own Colt as he did so.

The wagon was end-on, its canvas pulled across leaving only a narrow gap. It was for that gap that Jed Herne dived. He sprang off his right foot, grasping the top of the canvas and swinging his body through. A startled face was suddenly inches away from his own and he struck at it with his fist.

He rolled to one side, bringing up the gun he had taken from the dead Mexican. In the half light he saw two shapes jump out of the opposite end of the wagon. One more rose up a couple of feet away, somehow trying to turn a rifle through too small a space. Herne fired fast. The gun was less well balanced than his own, the shot taking the man in the forearm, smashing the bone.

Herne moved to his right to avoid the falling rifle and fired a second time. The Mexican went back against the side of the wagon, arms outstretched. The weight of his fall tore the canvas from the sides and he collapsed with it, finally clasping hold of one of the metal hoops of the frame.

While he hung there, blood welling from the centre of his chest, Herne turned to deal with the man he had punched. He was trying to burrow a way between the boxes of supplies on the floor. Herne jerked him up by his collar and only just managed to parry a thrust from the knife the man brought arcing up in his right hand.

Jed's left arm stopped the descent of the knife inches from his face, jamming against the man's wrist. At the same moment he discharged the pistol into his body.

The explosion was muffled by the closeness of the target. Herne felt the Mexican convulse against him and saw the head drop forward, the pupils thrust upwards in their sockets. The mouth shot open and a gout of blood flew out splattering Herne on his chin and neck.

He pushed the man off him, lifting his leg and kicking him off the wagon. He pushed the Mexican's gun down into his belt and wiped the blood and sweat off his face with the sleeve of his coat.

Coburn called out from the second wagon. 'Jed! You all right?'

'Sure am. You?'

'Yep. But one of your bastards got to the horses.'

Herne jumped down to the ground, reloading his Colt as he did so. He looked in the direction that Whitey was pointing. A man bent low over his saddle, whipping his mount hard, first one side then the other.

'Damn! And there's another.'

'Well where the . . .?'

The splash from the river gave them their answer.

Coburn ran towards the horses. 'I'd rather ride than swim,' he shouted. 'I'll be back.'

As Whitey vaulted on to the back of his horse and set off in pursuit of the Mexican, Herne turned towards the river. At the point where they had met Don Vincento and his men, it was running through a broad sweep and it was a good distance to the far shore.

Also, the current was quite strong.

Herne moved down to the bank, watching the arms come over and over, the head rising up on its right side only, gulping down air. Jed pulled off his coat and boots, then unbuckled his gun belt. He waded into the edge of the water, waiting until it was above his knees before he slid into a low dive.

Minutes later he was gaining on the Mexican, who had jumped in still wearing most of his clothes and was finding the going difficult. Herne swam steadily, never doubting he would overhaul him before he reached the middle of the river.

The Mexican began to glance back over his shoulder, panicking as he realized how close the American now was. He splashed frantically against the surface of the water, fighting it but always losing, expending his energy when he was about to need it most.

Only a couple of yards away now, Herne pushed against the current so that he could come into his man with extra force. His right arm rose from the water and fingers grabbed for the Mexican's long hair, yanking it from the back of his neck and pulling the head towards him.

The man struggled vainly, bringing his other arm round in an effort to free himself from Herne's grip. This sent him down below the surface of the river, legs kicking wildly as he knew the fear of death by drowning.

Herne held hard and tried to grasp the Mexican under water with his other hand, but the man's convulsions made that impossible. Finally Herne had to let go of the lank hair and wait for him to push up above the level of the water.

The head broke through the surface and Herne swung a punch at it. His fist landed on the side of the man's face and the head disappeared again. Only momentarily this time.

It burst back into the air, mouth open, eyes blinking. Herne's second punch missed, striking the water instead. The Mexican grabbed his hand and then his arm, pulling Herne towards him. Something stung at his side under the surface and Herne knew then that the Mexican was armed with a knife.

He struggled to free his arm and for several seconds both of them went under, only the turbulent movement above and a succession of air bubbles testifying to their presence.

Herne surfaced first, turning on to his back and kicking with his legs through the swirling water. The Mexican ducked away from the feet and his knife flashed brightly in the sun that had appeared above them.

Herne watched the blade fall and timed his dive back under. He rose fast, one hand bunched hard and tight and driving up between the Mexican's legs.

The pain from his side had begun to penetrate and he knew the struggle had to be finished and finished fast.

As the Mexican groaned and swallowed a mouthful of muddy water, Herne swung an arm into his face, driving him backwards. He leapt on top of him, forcing him down below the surface and searching for the hand that held the knife.

Legs threshed beneath him as the man fought for his life, struggling vainly to reach fresh air. Herne's fingers closed about the right wrist, squeezing and twisting, prising the handle of the knife clear.

For a second it floated free before Herne secured it.

He pushed himself backwards and caught his breath, waiting his moment. It was not long in coming.

No sooner had the Mexican gasped in a lungful of air than the blade ripped down into his throat, tearing at the flesh and cutting towards the windpipe. Herne pulled it away and cut downwards a second time, then a third.

Blood spread across the turbulence of the water and was tugged downstream by the current. The Mexican lay on his back, arms sideways, most of his head beneath the surface. The neck lay level with the top of the moving water, the skin cut and slashed apart so that a dark hole coughed blood like the open mouth of some hideous dying fish.

Herne plunged his face back down into the water then up again, clearing his eyes and his mind. The wound in his side was nothing now. He let the knife fall slowly towards the bed of the river then turned and struck out for the shore, away from the ever-widening circle of blood.

The Mexican in front of Coburn knew it was no use stopping and trying to fight the man off. Not a man as mad as that crazed one with white hair and those terrible eyes. He shuddered despite himself at the thought.

No, his only hope was to get to La Rosita before him. There he would be safe. And there he could find help.

He turned in his saddle and took a quick look behind; the Gringo was getting closer all the time. Vehemently, he whipped into his horse's flanks with the ends of the reins, lashing first one side and then the other. He ducked his head lower, so that it was along the animal's neck, close to the bouncing black hair of the mane. The smell of sweat filled his nose: the thunder of Coburn's pursuing horse filled his ears.

Whitey knew that his time was limited; knew also that the Mexican would not make the town unless some miracle saved him.

The Mexican drew his pistol and leaned his head and shoulders round, trying to steady his aim without slackening speed. Coburn heard the sound of the shot and saw the puff of smoke but the bullet missed him by yards. Then as the Mex tried a second time, Coburn's horse stumbled.

Whitey felt the juddering movement, the faltering stride. He cursed aloud and knew that the animal was about to lose its footing completely. As the second shot flew well wide, he grabbed at his Winchester and freed his feet from the stirrups. Better to jump than be thrown.

He checked the reins and moved his left leg high and ready.

Counted.

Jumped.

The earth seemed to spring up to meet him. He landed awkwardly, losing his grasp of the rifle and tumbled over and over, bruising his left shoulder.

Quickly he righted himself and seized the Winchester. The man he had been chasing was already a hundred yards away and getting smaller every second. Getting closer to La Rosita.

He knelt and pushed up the extra rear sight on the stock of the weapon. A hundred and thirty yards. And forty. Fifty.

The recoil slammed back into his shoulder and through the smoke of the explosion the Mexican seemed to be riding still. Then, as though in slow motion, he tumbled sideways from the saddle. His right boot caught in the stirrup and trailed him along for another twenty or thirty yards, banging his head and shoulders against the ground.

Finally he fell free and was still.

Whitey Coburn stood up and started to walk forward. His horse had started to hobble back in the direction it had come. He let it go. The Mexican's horse had stopped further along the trail and was cropping at one of the few patches of grass.

Fifty yards away and the Mexican had still not moved.

Most likely he was unconscious, winded. A pistol had fallen wide of his reach and was useless.

Coburn wasn't taking any chances. He covered the man all the way in with his Winchester, watching for any sign of movement.

Nothing.

He kicked the gun further away and came and stood behind the body. A trickle of blood came out from underneath the curved brim of the man's hat, where it lay over the back of his head.

Coburn kicked hard at the sole of one boot. 'Get up, you shammin' bastard!'

Still nothing.

'I said get your arse off'n that ground!'

Nothing again.

Coburn let the rifle fall back into his left hand and reached down with his right to pull the man round. As he did so, the Mexican sprang to life, pushing himself off the earth with surprising speed. A fist landed in Coburn's face and a boot went into his thighs, six inches below the groin. Coburn fell backwards, trying to swing the barrel of the rifle at the man but missing as he lost balance.

The Mexican's hand grabbed at his throat and squeezed hard, forcing themselves against his wind pipe and stopping the supply of air.

For what seemed a long time but was in reality no more than seconds, Coburn felt his lungs heaving for air that was not there. He closed his eyes as they began to bulge forward in his unnaturally pale face, the pupils pink and protruding. Everything went a sudden overwhelming black: a blackness which threatened to envelop him.

Then he rammed his left knee upwards hard, hard, harder!

The fingers on his throat loosened their grip. Enough to let Coburn gasp a quick breath. He opened his eyes and saw the strained face of the man above him. He spat upwards and kicked again at the same time.

Instinct freed one of the hands to wipe the spittle clear.

Coburn pivotted back on his buttocks and brought up both legs together. They took the Mexican in the pit of the stomach and lifted him high into the air.

Coburn jumped aside, one hand rubbing at his neck, the other grabbing at his holster. The Colt was missing. It had been shaken loose in the struggle, despite the loop usually tight around the hammer.

The Mexican had scrambled to his feet and was about to try yet again. Coburn braced himself and waited for the man to make his move.

There was a feint with the right and then the left hand going straight for the eyes, fingers extended. Coburn pulled his head back and knocked the arm upwards. He dropped his body fast and punched up into the man's belly. As the Mexican fell, Coburn was round and on his back, one arm tightening about his neck, the other chopping at the adam's apple.

Teeth bit deeply into his upper arm as the man managed to twist his head sideways. Coburn let go and jumped to one side.

The Mexican dived towards the gun that had been kicked away: there was no way in which he was going to get it.

Whitey let him sprawl, moving fast and stomping his boot heel down on to the rear of the man's knuckles. He waited as the shout faded and the face turned towards him, then kicked out again.

The toe of his right boot embedded itself savagely in the Mexican's startled face. There was a soft squelching followed closely by the cry of agony and the crunching of bone.

Coburn looked down at the face: he kicked it some more.

The edge of his heel caught against the top of the left eye socket and the man collapsed on to his back and showed no signs of moving again.

There wasn't any point in taking chances.

Coburn bent down and retrieved the Mexican's gun. He weighed it in his hand for a few moments, watching the blood wash over the man's face and the muscles of his arms and legs twitch involuntarily.

When he checked the chamber, there was one shell remaining. Whitey spun it across his left palm and pointed the barrel down at the man's chest.

He squeezed the trigger and the body bucked upwards as the bullet drove down and through it into the earth beneath.

'I guess,' said Coburn, 'it just ain't your lucky day.'

His voice was quiet and, in the vastness of the plain, strangely lost. Coburn tossed the pistol down by the Mexican's body and walked over towards where the man's horse was still munching unconcernedly.

## Chapter Eight

Jed Herne sat cross-legged on the ground eating from a plate of beef and beans. The meat had become rather charred on the outside edge, but it still tasted better than anything he had had inside him since he couldn't remember when. The beans were well spiced with chillies and he relished the burning sharpness on his palate.

He reached down and picked up a bottle of wine and swallowed deeply. It wasn't chilled any longer, but Herne had never been one to fuss about such things.

He hadn't been surprised when the Mexes had tried to take the money from him and keep what they were selling. Even so, he had allowed himself to get caught with both hands full and no easy way out. He was fast enough to have dropped plate and mug and get his Colt clear ... fast enough, but against two guns already cocked?

Herne shook his head and chewed thoughtfully. It was as well that Whitey had been there. A man almost as fast as himself. Almost?

Jed grinned. He didn't know. Had no way of being certain. Come to that, he didn't want to know. Like he'd said to the man back in that saloon, he sure as hell wouldn't like to have to live on the difference.

Only that was what he had lived on today – Coburn's speed of thought and action. And not for the first time.

Whenever they had worked together, each man backed up the other naturally, covering and watching, a perfect team.

In those days when he had been travelling across the country with Becky and Whitey had been leading a group of men after him, it had not been right.

Neither of them had ever said as much, but both had known: it had felt wrong. All wrong.

Whitey Coburn was his friend: that was the way it was.

Jed looked up from his food at the sound of a horse approaching.

He set his fork down on the plate and drifted his hand towards the Colt at his thigh. He could tell that the animal was not trotting evenly. Most likely lame in one leg. Neither did it seem to be carrying a rider.

The Colt slid from its holster and Herne stood up, placing the food on the ground by his left foot. It was Whitey's horse, sure enough. The saddle empty.

Herne watched as the animal came towards the wagons, the bodies, the fire. Its front leg on the right side was barely touching the earth as it moved.

Behind it, the horizon was bare.

Jed Herne thought again of his friend, of Whitey's wishes to settle down along of a river much like this one. Only lusher, greener land. A small ranch. A woman. A little gold, maybe. Enough to see its colour against the markings of a hand that had lived by a gun.

As he stood there, a fresh sound broke into his mind. A second horse, coming faster, more directly – with a rider.

Herne waited, alert. Almost, he didn't want to look. He looked. In the end all sentimentality got you was dead before your time.

Yet something stirred within him when he saw the albino's long white hair moving in the wind; something he would never show.

'Where you bin?' he asked as Coburn slid down from his saddle.

'Takin' care of business.'

Herne looked him over. 'Seems like it took care of you, near enough.'

Coburn shrugged: 'I'm okay.' He looked about him. 'You?'

'Uh-huh. Scratch on my side. Get yourself some of that chow. Then we better check our load and move out. Reckon we might find ourselves gettin' company afore we reach the border.'

Coburn raised an eyebrow and went over to the dying fire, preparing to take meat. 'That's too bad.'

'Yep.'

For a while both men ate in silence. Then Coburn's eyes drifted towards the still shape of Don Vincento, less than ten yards behind them.

'That bastard's startin' to stink already.'

Herne gave a short laugh. 'I guess he didn't smell so sweet before.'

'What was that he said? Something about a man who shares his meat with another won't never spill his blood?'

'Somethin' like that.'

Coburn spat a mouthful of gristle at the dead man's face. What had been his face. 'I knew that fat bastard reminded me of that damned cock I took the head off.'

Herne nodded and stood up, dropping the plate down with a clatter. 'You ready?'

'All but.'

Coburn stepped past the dead Mexican leader and paused to bend over something on the ground. 'Jesus Christ! Will you take a look at this?'

The grey mess that had been shot away through the back of Don Vincento's skull still lay where it had fallen, partly on tin, partly on the ground. But where before it had been flecked with his blood, it was now alive with a mass of insects, black, red and brown. They moved over every square inch, a slowly buzzing, shifting morass of carnivorous greed.

Herne stared down. 'They know what's good for 'em. Best part of the body to eat, some say.'

Coburn stood straight. 'Hope it does them a sight more good than it did him. Bastard had more brains than was good for him.'

He kicked hard at the plate and it bounced down to the edge of the riverbank. Herne was already over by the wagon, checking one of the boxes.

They were wooden crates, tied each way with strong rope. Thirty of them, stacked in threes. Herne lifted one of them down to the ground, cursing it for being so heavy.

He drew the bayonet from his boot and cut through the rope at one side. He pulled at the wood with his hands but it was nailed down too securely.

'Whitey! Fetch somethin' to lever this off with.'

Coburn pulled at one end of the metal posts that had been used for the spit and brought it over. Within moments the crate was open and Herne was lifting away the straw that had been used for packing.

He lifted out a squat, heavy statue and held it up. It was a badly formed figure sitting in front of what might have been a representation of the sun. The clay had been baked hard; the colour a dull, dark brown.

'No wonder that Mex was laughing his balls off if all them crates are full of junk like that.'

'If.'

The two men tried several crates at random. There were bowls by the dozen, mostly painted with birds or animals at the centre of odd geometric designs. Coburn lifted out one with a painting of a pregnant woman, legs spread wide apart and both hands holding her private parts exaggeratedly open. He whistled.

'Jesus! A man could get lost in there and never touch the sides!'

They found small shell ornaments shaped like birds or lizards; jars with handles decorated with black and white swirls; purse-like objects fashioned from bone; glazed black waters jars; tiny dolls less than three inches tall.

But nothing else.

The cargo was what it appeared to be. Even at half the original asking price it seemed damned expensive.

But that wasn't Herne's worry. Getting it across the border into Texas was.

'Whitey,' he said as the tops of the crates were hammered into place.

'Yep?'

'If my guess is right, they'll be expectin' us to head for the border by the closest route. More or less the way we came in.'

'Which we ain't about to do?'

'Right. If'n we ride south and cross the river lower down, we can take a trail east and get into Texas south of Laredo.'

Coburn set the last crate back into place and wiped his forehead. 'They'll come lookin' for us?'

'When someone takes it into his head to find out what happened to that Vincento, they'll come a-plenty. For one thing, they'll know we've got money. For a second, we done killed eight of their own kind. If you want another reason, it's 'cause they think us Gringos are goin' t' attack in strength that their part of the country's kept the way it is.'

Herne sniffed and spat. 'Any one of them damned reasons'd do.'

'Okay. We'd better pick up whatever weapons and ammo we can find an' load 'em on this wagon. If we're goin' t' get ourselves chased by a damned army of rebels, we might as well get as prepared as we can.'

As soon as the river was out of sight, the land petered out into near-desert. Whitey rode up in the wagon, while Jed Herne kept on his own mount. Every now and then he would swing away, riding on ahead or round. Anywhere he might find a useful vantage point. Anything that looked capable of holding an ambush.

They had taken two spare horses from among the Mexicans' string and these were tied to the rear of the wagon, along with Coburn's own black. Its leg had not been badly damaged and if the animal did not have to take a rider for a while it might mend of its own accord.

The ground was a dull yellow under the equally dull sun. Eccentric shapes of cactus stuck up at intervals along with incongruously bright desert flowers. What trees there were appeared stunted, mostly scrubby firs set on slight rises of land.

It had become less cold: the turn of fall into winter heralded by a false promise of real warmth.

It was something you never really knew, thought Herne as he headed back in towards the wagon – the moment when the seasons changed. All that waiting and then next thing you knew it had already happened.

He guessed it was much like waiting for death.

His eyes focussed on Whitey on the wooden seat, his Winchester standing close beside him, butt to the floor. Yep, you never knew. Just got the feelin' when it was close. Like the shiver down your spine for no good reason.

'Nothin'?' Coburn asked.

Herne shook his head. 'Only a lot more of the same.'

Coburn bit of a piece of tobacco and began to chew furiously. There was nothing else to do; nothing to say. They could only keep heading for the border.

They damned near made it.

It was early the following day and Herne was standing in his stirrups close by a pair of firs with short, stubby branches. Ahead of him he could see the wavering line where the vegetation altered. The desert gave way to green and he knew that that green led to the river and the border.

Below him, moving at the same steady pace they had adopted since leaving, was the wagon, its three horses trotting behind.

And behind, rising like a thick cloud into the sky, was the dust of men riding fast. Many men.

Herne looked quickly around. Apart from the spot he was on, there was nothing that rose above the same cursed flatness. Not a shred of cover anywhere.

He inserted two fingers in his mouth and whistled twice. The first note going up, the second descending.

Coburn responded to the signal. The pair of horses pulling the wagon were halted; his Winchester was checked and ready by the time Herne had ridden down to join him.

'Yep?'

'Signs of men headin' this way. A whole crowd of 'em. Must be at least twenty from the dust they're sendin' up. Could be more.'

'Comin' for us?'

Herne gestured about them. 'Can you see anyone else they're likely to be after?'

Coburn grunted and chewed all the harder. 'Any cover?'

'Not a damned thing.'

'Bastard country!'

'I see it this way. You move the wagon deeper in and we'll get those crates down and back of her. Then set it over on its side. If you stay there and use that for cover, I'll hightail it back up to them trees an' pick off a few as they come in.'

'Ain't you goin' t' get yourself trapped up there?'

'That's my problem. Anyhow, seems better than gettin' us both pinned down rear of this wagon. An' there's no way we're goin' to to outrun 'em.'

'Right. Let's move it!'

They got the crates down as fast as they could, the knife wound in Herne's side nagging at him as the effort stretched and opened it once more. When the wagon was on its side, Whitey collected the guns they had taken and set them in a line close to hand.

'Take care,' he called as Herne rode off.

Jed's reply was lost in the distance between them.

Herne used his rope to secure the horse some way back of the firs, hoping that it would not get hit by a stray bullet. He lay flat on the rough ground, his Sharps stretched out in front of him, watching the dust cloud grow larger, nearer. The dark blur at its centre broke into separate shapes. Men and mounts: still too far off to count how many.

Coburn could see the first signs now. He inserted a fresh plug of tobacco into his mouth and leaned his cheek against the smooth stock of the Winchester. To his right there were three more rifles – a lever-action .44 Henry, a Winchester .44 carbine with the barrel a good six inches shorter than his own, lastly an English-made Kerr, a .44 calibre weapon the Confederacy had used as a sniper's rifle in the Civil War.

Beyond them lay four pistols: a Colt similar to his own; a self-cocking .44 Starr; a pair of Smith and Wesson Schofield .45s.

Wherever the Mexicans had been buying their arms from, they had surely got themselves a varied supply.

All of the weapons were loaded and ready. Nothing now but the waiting. Coburn's mind went back to the eighteen-sixties. Times out of number he'd been wedged under wagons then, taking pot shots at Apaches as they rode round in some damned circle, or charged in and over the top. Country much like this now . . .

Years later it had been the Lincoln County Range War. More blasted wagons. More waiting. Jed had been along of him then. Around the time they met Billy; the one they called the Kid; the one as Pat Garrett shot in Pete Maxwell's bedroom.

'Quien es?' Billy was supposed to have said.

'Quien es?'

Poor bastard found out soon enough! Poor mad bastard!

He moved his weight on to his other side and stared ahead, past the end of the wagon.

The riders had spread themselves out now, sufficient for Herne to make a better count. Thirty was closer than twenty. He sighted along the top of the Sharps, moving the barrel so slowly from right to left that it seemed no movement at all.

He levelled on one man close to the centre, letting the shape fill out inside the V. Something less than six hundred yards, he reckoned. His finger squeezed the trigger nice and easy. Come on, you beauty! Come on!

As he held the rifle steady, the rider disappeared from between its sights. Herne saw the men on either side of him shift away; the line broke, startled. By the time it had re-formed, he had slid another shell into the breech.

Moved down the line to the right.

Fired.

Allowed himself a wry smile.

Reloaded.

He got off eight shots inside the first minute. Six of them struck home. One missed altogether as the target swung aside as the trigger was pulled back. Another hit a horse on a line between its eyes.

Herne cursed himself bitterly for that. Not that he was upset about the animal – but that he had missed his man for no good reason.

Time enough for them to regroup into three, one swinging to the far side of the trees which picked out Herne's position, the others riding in on the wagon.

Time also for Coburn to have them within range. He tried a shot with his Winchester and a Mexican toppled sideways in his saddle, hands tight upon the pommel, hanging on for his life. Coburn followed him round and pumped the lever. The second shot took him high in the chest and the fingers released their hold.

He swung the rifle in the other direction and fired round after round quickly, going for speed rather than accuracy, driving the closest group aside, apart.

Having emptied the Winchester, he let it fall and reached for the Henry.

Herne had shifted his position and lay now with his body

sideways on to the main attacking force, the Sharps pointing down towards the group that had cut away to attack him.

He had already dropped two of them and was aiming at a third. He saw an arm go up, the sombrero flip backwards, held by the cord about its owner's neck.

Enough.

He pushed another shell home and fired instantaneously. A Mexican dropped his gun, shot through the arm. He kept coming. Herne ignored him and found one of the others in his sights. This time the bullet hammered into the middle of the Mexican's chest, smashing the breast bone to fragments. The man's legs spread wide, feet jerked from the stirrups. As his mount rode on, he seemed for a second suspended, riding the air.

Herne didn't wait to see him fall. He knew.

Load and fire. Load and fire again.

Then there was only one man left in the saddle and that the one he had shot in the arm. He was pulling a pistol from his belt with his left hand, grimacing with pain. Herne could see his face clearly; eyes surprisingly blue, mouth set firm and thin.

Herne stood up fast, Sharps in his left hand. He drew his Colt and fired in a single movement. The hand on the Mexican's gun released its hold. Lids came down over the blue eyes. The man was dead before he had dropped from the saddle.

A shot ricocheted off the tree to Herne's right. He turned swiftly, gun still in hand, crouching low. A second shot went close enough to his head for him to feel the wind of it.

Two of the Mexicans had come up behind him on foot. They had made their chance and then thrown it away – like their lives.

Herne shot the man to his right high in the chest and watched as he threw up his pistol high towards the sky and wheeled round fast.

Before the gun had started its descent the second man was

clutching at a death wound in his throat and Herne had holstered his own Colt.

Below him some dozen Mexicans were riding round the lone wagon, firing at the figure of Whitey Coburn, jammed down alongside its wheels and base.

Herne picked off one with his Sharps, then ran for his horse. He jumped from several feet away, one foot slotting accurately into the stirrup, a hand pulling the rope free.

As the animal moved, he pushed back down on the ground with his right boot, twice, three times, then swung into the saddle. Coburn saw him coming out the corner of one eye. There was no time for more than a hasty glance. Two of the attackers were coming straight for him, firing wildly as they rode.

Whitey fired the Henry from the hip and saw one rock backwards; he pressed the trigger a second time and nothing happened. The blasted thing had jammed!

Coburn threw himself to the ground and started to roll sideways, clawing for his Colt as he went. He was vaguely aware of the Mexican high over him and heard the explosion of his pistol. He rolled further and came up to his knees. The man was still there. Coburn pulled out his gun and fired upwards.

The man was already dead.

Herne had shot him through the side of his head, just below the line of his wide-brimmed hat. He jumped from his horse and landed six feet away from Coburn.

'What kept you?'

'Wanted to see if you could handle it on your own.'

Coburn's reply was lost in a volley of gunfire. They were moving in for a final attack.

The two Americans steadied themselves, facing in opposite directions. Each using pistols now for closer range. Steady, controlled firing. The Mexicans, shaken at having their force cut down so dramatically, shot in desperation and fear. Against the pair of professionals it was not enough.

Three more dead or dying. One got close enough to throw himself from the back of his horse on to Herne's kneeling body. Jed caught at the man's arm and turned him over fast, dropping a knee hard into his groin. His right hand reached down to his boot and pulled out the bayonet he kept sheathed there.

There was a flash of terrified recognition in the Mexican's dark eyes at the long blade drove in under his ribs and penetrated the heart.

Herne stood up and looked about him. Whitey Coburn was earnestly pushing fresh shells into the smoking chambers of his Colt. The two men looked at one another and nodded slowly. It was all right again.

As they moved amongst the dead and dying there was a terrible silence, broken only by the flapping of carrion wings from the topmost branch of a nearby tree.

## Chapter Nine

They had been to Laredo before. Many times. And on each visit the place seemed somehow different. The shacks and shanties round the outskirts had spread; many that had been there before were falling down and simply being left to rot. Now kids and mangy curs ran in amongst them in an interminable game of chase.

The centre of the town had thickened out. Grown up in more ways than one.

Where there had once been single storeyed buildings with huge false fronts, they now had genuine two and three floors. A dentist hung his sign above the property of Davies, Jackson and Co., purveyors of General Merchandise. The Champion Boot and Shoe Maker of Texas shared a building with one Elwood P. Travers, specialist in Fire Arms and Ammunition. A poster showing a pair of straight boots coloured a vivid red was above one for the new Smith and Wesson, carved handle pistol.

Two doors down from the Laredo Star saloon was Zelda's Fun Palace, with girls hanging their heads and bare shoulders from nearly every window.

Herne and Coburn rode past all of this, taking it in with interest, yet never allowing it to distract them from the possibility of danger. In a town where folk would know them and where their reputation would still be a source for gossip and bragging in the saloons and bars, there could well be somebody drunk enough, puffed up sufficiently with false pride, to call them out. Even to try a shot at their backs.

But they reached the livery stables without incident.

The man who limped down to greet them winced visibly as he set his foot to the ground at the bottom of the ladder from the loft. He pushed the pain back from his face and a wave of recognition took its place.

'Dang me! It ain't . . .?'

Herne grinned and stepped quickly forward clasping the man by the hand and clapping him enthusiastically on his shoulder. 'Bin a long time, Larry. Half thought you might have upped and gone.'

The livery man shook his head and the frayed ends of whitening hair bounced around the bald spot that dominated his skull. He patted his hands across his broad spreading stomach and smiled. 'Only one place I'd be goin', Jed, an' that's six foot under. No mistake.'

He laughed again and Herne looked at him, finding it hard to accept that Larry and himself were much of an age. Had run together way back when. One night Herne had been facing three outlaws in the main street right there in Laredo. Larry had been backing him up with an old single shot Richmond Sharps. He'd been mighty proud of that rifle – carried it ever since the Shenandoah Valley. That particular night it hadn't done him a lot of good; not for the first time the mechanism had fouled.

Larry had taken a bullet high in the left thigh and another lower down in the same leg.

The doc had got all of one of them out and most of the other. The fragments that were left still bit at his flesh whenever it rained, as soon as winter began to set in.

Herne noticed he was favouring the leg now.

'Turnin' raw?'

Larry nodded and rubbed the thigh openly. 'Damn right! Blasted thing that it is!'

Jed Herne knew. Knew also that had he stopped those bullets that night he might have been the one to have stayed in Laredo and taken on work in the livery stable. Instead of which . . .

'You an' your friend seem to be well loaded.'

Herne knew the man was aware of Coburn and his name of Whitey, but was hesitant to use it. 'Reckon you can find a space for this wagon of ours? Somewhere out back where it won't be too noticeable. Horses, too.'

'Yep. Though now you've ridden her through town it don't seem to matter much where you put her. Ain't too many secrets kept in a place like this.'

'I know that.'

Larry looked at the bullet marks and holes in the wagon's woodwork. 'Looks to me like you got somethin' in there folk bin tryin' powerful hard to get their hands on.'

'They ain't got near it yet,' interrupted Coburn abruptly, his voice harsh. 'Not here neither.' He stared at the livery man hard and long.

'Tell him he don't have to worry none about me, Jed. You tell him that. Tell him 'bout the time . . .'

Herne laid a hand on him again. 'It's all right, Larry. I know it's safer with you than most. But if you could keep a special eye open . . . for old time's sake.'

Larry grinned and patted the gun at his side. 'Don't worry, Jed. No bastard's goin' t' get his nose even near that there wagon of yorn. Not while I'm about, he ain't.'

'Thanks, Larry. You always was a good man.'

When Herne and Coburn were at the livery stable door, the bald man called after them: 'If'n you get up to Zelda's – give them blasted girls one for me.'

Jed waved and they walked out into the main street, leaving Larry with his chuckling dreams.

A couple of hours later the two men had got themselves a room in Ma Carey's Boarding House and were sitting in a pair of new enamel hip baths at the rear of the Laredo Bathhouse and Barber Shop, Greene and Ross, proprietors.

Jed splashed the soapy water up underneath his armpits and then reached down to the floor and picked up the glass of whiskey he had sent out for special. Whitey rested his arms on the sides of the tub, his head back, a long cigar stuck out from his mouth, the occasional wisps of smoke merging with the steam of the room.

The curtain was pulled aside and Rosie Ross appeared, a wooden bucket in one hand. 'Either of you gents needin' hottin' up?'

Coburn opened one eye. 'You could come over here and rub a little soap over my back. That'd warm me up some.' The eye winked, then closed again.

He knew well enough she wasn't about to take him up on it and so did she.

'I'll take a little of that,' said Jed, a moment later enjoying the surge of warmth that ran down his back and sides and up between his legs. He glanced up at Rosie, at the dark eyes and fleshy arms.

There'd been a time when she had done a sight more than soap his naked body and it had been good. It had also been a long time ago.

'Jed,' her voice was soft and she spoke as she still leant over the tub, 'some feller's bin askin' round town for you.'

Herne tensed slightly. 'What kind of feller?'

'Small. Half-breed by the look of him. Dressed pretty fancy.'

Herne nodded.

'You know him?' her forearm was almost touching his shoulder now and he could feel her warmth.

'Could be.'

'Pete says he saw him close by the end of town talking to a man named Charlie Whitten.'

Herne shook his head.

'He's a wastrel hangs round town. Picks up work where he can. Thinks he's good with a gun.'

Herne fixed Rosie with a firm look. 'Is he?'

The brown eyes smiled: 'Not once he's put up against you, he ain't?'

Herne returned the smile. 'Thanks, Rosie.'

She stood up, picked up the bucket and walked out of the room.

Coburn stirred in the bath, breaking the surface of scum that had formed. 'You two was havin' a real nice talk,' he grinned, the cigar still smouldering in his mouth.

'She didn't say the name, but I reckon as how Thursby's in town. An' he's askin' for us.'

Whitey removed the cigar from his mouth. 'Is that a fact? Well now . . . well now . . .'

He lay back once more and settled his back against the smooth enamel. If Antonio Thursby had come looking for them, they surely weren't about to hide.

The half-breed found them in the eating house down the street. Both men had been shaved and Jed had let the barber lop an inch or two off his hair. They were wearing clean shirts and feeling pretty damned good. Relaxed.

Two large t-bone steaks had just been served on oval plates, along with potatoes and beans and thick slices of bread. After they had each taken a mouthful Thursby stepped forward.

'Ah, gentlemen. So pleasant to see you again.'

Neither man answered, but carried on chewing.

Thursby took another pace forward, a little hesitant now. He was wearing a dark suit with a light grey waistcoat and a silver watch chain that hung in two loops across its front.

'I trust – er – your little mission has proved successful.'

Whitey chewed some more, spat a piece of gristle down on to the floor and finally looked up. 'That little mission you're talkin' about cost a lot of men's lives – an' that's just so far.'

Thursby tried to avoid looking back into the pink eyes, but it was difficult. He tried to avoid the threat in Coburn's voice, but that was impossible.

'Well, at least both of you gentlemen are in one piece. I . . .'

'No damned thanks to you!'

'But . . .'

Herne spoke softly, firmly. 'How much you agree to pay for them pots?'

Thursby went as white as he was able. 'I . . . you know . . .'

Coburn banged his knife down hard on the table. 'You're damned right, we know!'

He was halfway up from his seat when the door at the side of the eating house was pushed open and slammed loudly back against the wall. The man who stepped through was about the same build as Jed Herne. He wore a flat brimmed hat with a white cord dangling below his chin. Black shirt and pants. A scowl screwed up one side of his face and he leant his body to the left so that the knuckles of his left hand grazed the butt of his gun.

Coburn stared at the man, then looked across the table at Herne.

'Shit!' he said, his voice a mixture of disbelief and disgust.

'Everything okay, Mr. Thursby?' the newcomer asked.

'Er, yes. Yes, Charlie.'

'Sure, Charlie,' said Coburn standing straight and pushing the chair well clear of the table. 'But you stick around. When I've finished my steak I just might throw you the bone.'

Charlie Whitten's scowl grew deeper and the hand stopped moving on the gun.

Thursby hopped nervously from one foot to the other and back again. Herne did nothing. Said nothing. Waited.

'See, gentlemen, it's like this. I've got the rest of your money here with me.' His hand moved to the front of his coat and Herne rested his own hand on his Colt. 'I will personally take charge of the merchandise here and relieve you of your – er – duties.'

He looked expectantly from Herne to Coburn and back

again. Neither man showed anything in his face. Neither spoke.

The fingers reached deeper. 'Well then, gentlemen, I presume that matter is agreed . . .'

Coburn stepped forward fast and grabbed hold of the man's hand and the front of his waistcoat at the same time. He lifted him clear of the ground and sat him down on an adjacent table, clattering the knives and forks to the floor.

By the door, Charlie Whitten had drawn his pistol halfway out of its holster when he realized that Herne's Colt was pointing at his chest. He froze fast, mouth open and eyes wide.

Thursby was spluttering with outrage – until Coburn slapped him twice about his swarthy face, drawing blood from the edge of his mouth.

'Right!' Whitey said menacingly. 'You didn't answer our question. How much was we supposed to give to those damned Mexes?'

'Five thousand,' the half-breed squealed.

Coburn hit him again. With his fist this time and full in the centre of his face. Thursby's nose spouted blood down his neat, grey waistcoat.

'How much?'

'Five thousand,' the little man all but sobbed.

He winced and fell forward as Coburn punched him in the stomach. Whitey sidestepped neatly and Thursby's head smacked the floor with a sharp crack that echoed around the dining-room.

The waitress appeared in the doorway, took one look and went hastily away again. Whitten was still staring down the barrel of Herne's .45. He didn't seem to like it, but then he didn't seem to have a whole lot of choice.

Thursby tried to get up, but only succeeded in rolling over on to his side. He curled up into himself like a hedgehog in danger.

'Get up, you half-breed bastard!'

Thursby didn't move. Coburn kicked him in the head. He shrieked and scrambled towards the wall. Coburn reached down and lifted him high into the air, wheeling him round in a half circle and finally ramming him up against the wall opposite, feet well clear of the ground.

'Now let's get this straight. We got down into Mexico and found they was expectin' twice what you'd said. When we offered them the five thousand you give us, they wasn't pleased. Before we could get that junk of yorn out of there we had to fight off practically the whole of some damned rebel army. An' I didn't like that. I don't take to the idea of gettin' shot up on account of your twistin' and connivin'. You understand me?'

Thursby nodded, his eyes darkly spread with terror.

'Another thing,' interrupted Herne, talking over his shoulder and still covering the gunman at the door. 'We ain't about to hand over nothin' to you and your friend here. Less'n it's a couple of shells apiece. Our deal was to take that wagon to New Orleans and that's what we're goin' t' do. Whatever you're tryin' to cheat your partner out of, that's your business. Just don't expect to get us mixed up in it.'

'There was no intention to cheat . . .'

Coburn dropped him to the floor and the jolt made him stumble awkwardly forward.

'I think you've finished your business here,' Whitey said.

'Reckon that's so,' echoed Herne.

Antonio Thursby looked at his hired gun expectantly. But it was obvious that Charlie Whitten wasn't about to do anything other than get out of there as soon as he could.

Thursby walked to the door, slowly at first, finally scuttling through like a small animal. Whitten followed him and slammed the door shut behind him.

Herne holstered his gun and Coburn came back round to the table. The food on their plates was already a deal colder than it should have been, but they ate it with gusto.

'D'you think he'll try anythin' else?' Coburn asked, his mouth crammed with meat.

Jed shook his head. 'I don't reckon. After you scarin' the shit out of him like that, he's not goin' t' be in a hurry to tangle with us again.'

'Uum.'

The pair of them carried on with their meal, trying to get back to the feeling of well-being they had enjoyed before being interrupted.

It wasn't often that Herne was guilty of an error of judgement, but his assessment of Antonio Thursby's reactions had been far from correct.

The girl laying alongside Herne said her name was Tina. It probably wasn't, but that didn't matter. It was simply something to call out at those times when you had to yell someone's name and didn't want to dredge one from your memory.

So Tina it had been. Tina when she had arched herself underneath him, pale skin reflecting the moonlight sliding in through the window. Tina when she had swung herself on top of him and slithered smoothly down his hard body, gathering him in her warm mouth, red hair falling across his belly. Tina now as she lay inside the crook of his arm, his fingers gently stroking her bare breast.

She felt him tense as footsteps came within earshot along the corridor outside.

'Don't worry,' she said, 'it'll be one of the other girls.'

But his hand was already on the butt of his Colt and his nerves were fully awake. Through the window, the moon had been replaced by the first light of the sun.

The steps halted outside the door: Herne cocked his gun.

The girl pushed herself against his chest.

'Jed?'

It was Whitey's voice.

'Come on in if'n you must.'

The door opened and a grinning albino stood there, all dressed and ready to go.

Tina pulled the sheet up over her breasts and tried hard not to stare at the man who had come into the room.

'You done finished here?' Coburn asked.

'Guess so.'

Herne glanced down at the girl and moved his arm away from her. She turned her back on him and curled her legs up towards her stomach. Herne swung his legs over the edge of the bed and caught his long johns as Whitey threw them from the chair by the door.

Within a few minutes he was ready. He looked down at the girl, who still hadn't moved. Herne shrugged his shoulders and walked out of the small room with Whitey following.

On the street the early morning air struck cold on their faces, like the slap of an angry hand.

# Chapter Ten

Herne started running twenty yards this side of the livery stable: there were tracks in the dirt of the street which shouldn't have been there. Heavy wagon tracks.

Whitey hadn't been the only one up early that morning.

Where the wagon had been the day before, now there was nothing but space and scuffed footmarks.

'Larry?' asked Coburn.

'I don't know.'

Herne found him wedged between two bales of straw. They had been careful not to risk waking too many people. Someone had used a knife on him. There was a stab wound in his back, inches to the right of his spine. The blood around it had not yet dried, the coat and shirt matted together.

When Herne turned him over, the limbs had not yet set into the hardness of death. Not that that made any difference to Larry.

The knife had slashed at his throat as well, carving through the skin from the right ear down to beneath the chin. Ends of straw and dust clung to the congealed blood that ran along either side of the wound.

His hair fell over his head, partly concealing his bald patch. Somehow he looked younger than he had when he was alive.

Only one place for me to go, he had said. And already he was more or less there.

Herne sensed Coburn close behind him and the same

shiver of coldness he had felt before swept up through his loins.

'You reckon he tried to stop them?'

'Said he would. Larry was the kind of man always kept his word.' He looked at Coburn and there was a shadow deep in his eyes. 'He kept it best as he could.'

Coburn turned and stepped past the end bale. 'I'll get the horses fed and watered. They won't have gone so far we can't catch 'em easy.'

'Yep. I got somethin' to do first. It ain't goin' t' take long.'

He bent over Larry's body and straightened it, resting it gently down on to one of the straw bales. He picked the dirt from around his neck and laid the man's hands across his chest.

'Thanks, Larry,' he said quietly. 'Thanks for both times.'

He turned quickly and walked out of the stables, heading back up the street.

Rosie Ross didn't take any too kindly to being woken early from her sleep, but when Jed told her what had happened she softened some. He gave her enough money to pay for a decent burial and turned away.

'This ain't like you,' she said to his back.

Herne's face was drawn and lean. 'He was a friend of mine.'

Rosie spoke again when he was some way away. 'That's likely what got him killed,' she said.

If Jed Herne heard her he gave no sign.

'Seems to me they must know we're goin' t' come ridin' after 'em.'

'Yep.'

'An' good and angry, too.'

'Yep.'

'Angry enough to ride slap into an ambush.'

'Yep.'

The terrain was uneven, stretches of open plain broken up

by runnels and canyons. Thick valleys of woodland that spread themselves more thinly up the slopes. Woods whose trees were now mostly showing bare branches, their floors a mass of multi-coloured leaves.

Herne rode steadily between a line of tall alders, the bottom of his wool coat hitched up above the butt of his Colt.

Coburn came fifteen yards behind him, eyes flickering from left to right and back again, his own gun transferred from its holster to his belt. The handle stuck through the gap between the buttonholes of his coat. His right hand rested on the saddle pommel, reins between his middle fingers.

They had followed the tracks of the wagon, taking it slow and careful, waiting for the ambush both were certain Thursby would have set up.

It was the only way it made any sense.

Herne turned the upper half of his body in the saddle, looking quickly behind. A single leaf, golden brown, tumbled lazily down through the air and settled on the side of Coburn's white hair, clinging there.

The albino put up his hand and brushed it away.

Above them a flight of birds headed for warmer lands.

Herne moved round and looked at the trail ahead.

A quarter of a mile further on the trees finished suddenly and the horizon seemed to dip away. The sky was a dull grey filling the space before them.

Herne yawned and stretched his left arm out sideways, holding his body taut and straining it backwards against the rear of his saddle.

The crack of the rifle shot exploded into the middle of the yawn and Herne's horse stumbled to one side as though kicked hard. Almost instantly, he felt the warm pump of blood on to his thigh. The shell had missed him by an inch or less and had struck his mount through its side.

Behind him he heard Coburn shout and then there was a great crash as two trees fell to the ground, cutting off their path at both ends. Herne's horse went down on to its front legs.

He grabbed at the rifle and leapt clear before it keeled over completely, looking about him for signs of the ambushers. Another shot whistled close by him, kicking up the dirt just beyond and spraying it high in the air. He tucked himself in alongside the horse as two more bullets smacked into its flesh.

Coburn had jumped down and whipped his horse towards the trees at the side. His Winchester in his left hand, he had fired three shots with his Colt, covering himself before straddling the tree that had scarcely finished quivering behind him. A bullet rang out in answer and skidded off the trunk, tearing away a strip of bark as it went.

Coburn dived for the far side of the tree and pushed three fresh shells into his gun.

Herne, meanwhile, had picked out where some of the shots were coming from. A sniper, high up on a tree opposite, was standing on a stout branch, his rifle leaning on another.

Herne watched again for the flash, peering over the palpitating, bleeding body of his horse. He rested his right wrist on his left arm and fired. Once was enough.

There was a startled cry then the man came crashing down, bouncing off several branches before being buried in a welter of leaves at the bottom.

Herne guessed that left three or four more, at least. His thoughts were interrupted by firing from behind. So, they were both sides of the trail.

'Whitey!'

His shout was loud in the sudden silence of the wood.

'Yeah?'

'I'm shiftin' out of here.'

'Okay.'

Five seconds later Herne was on the move, ducking low and running for the group of trees that had concealed the sniper. The way he saw it, they would only have left one man on that side.

For the second time in two days he was wrong.

As Whitey's covering fire sang out behind him, he rushed in between two of the alders and put up his hand to shield his eyes from a low-hanging bough. Instantly, a short man with a pistol in his left hand sprang up in front of him as if from nowhere. Herne fired as he ran and the face disappeared as quickly as it had materialized. But not so quickly that the man did not get off one shot.

A line of pain cut across the top of Herne's right arm as the shell lanced through the skin and flesh at his left shoulder, grazing the bone.

He gasped and threw himself to the floor, rolling through the yellow and brown leaves to the shelter of a massive trunk.

Coburn was still firing and Herne could hear the differing tones of Colt and Winchester alternating. He tried to judge where the rest of the firing was coming from. He thought there were three different weapons being used on the other side of the trail, one of them a carbine.

There was also a gunman through the trees to his left.

Herne began to circle round behind him, taking care not to warn of his approach. He guessed their attackers were thrown into confusion by the immediate failure of their plan.

The intention was obvious: drop the trees, thereby hemming the two riders in. The distance Herne and Coburn had kept between them had made that difficult and probably widened their firing angle too greatly. The sniper was meant to take out the front man and had only marginally failed. Maybe that had made those who aimed at Coburn nervous.

Herne stopped. The head of his target showed a couple of inches of thick reddish hair above a broken stump of tree, then bobbed down again.

Beyond him, there was a flash of white as Coburn glanced

from his own shelter and snapped off a shot at the far side of the woods. It was returned threefold.

Herne moved forward, shifting the Colt to his left hand and levering the bayonet up from his boot. His boots trod down the leaves evenly, softly.

At the final moment the man whirled round: they usually did.

He met the end of the blade as it went in under the rib cage and pushed upwards for the lungs: Herne's favourite target. The other hand clubbed down, the corner of the gun butt driving into the top of the man's skull. His shout was cut off by the speed with which that blow jammed his mouth closed.

Herne extracted the blade which came out with a soft sighing sound. He wiped it on the man's pants and pushed him out of the way with his boot. From behind the stump he could see past Coburn into the trees on the other side of the trail.

As he readied himself a shot from Whitey's Colt produced a scream of pain and the sound of falling from that direction. Two remaining. He whistled their double note signal to let Coburn know where he was and listened to the reply.

Coburn began to fire more steadily and Herne watched as one of the attackers shifted his position backwards, edging out from behind a tree trunk, exposing himself to a danger he was unaware existed.

Herne showed him better.

The shot hit him low in the back and felled him as easily as a sapling.

The last man shouted out to his friends. His friend. There was no reply.

A moment later Herne and Coburn heard running, crashing sounds going deeper into the wood.

Coburn showed himself warily, then more boldly. 'Don't see him comin' back for more. He's goin' through them woods like a buck on heat.'

Herne got up and walked over to where Coburn was waiting. 'If we take a look around I think we'll find their horses tied somewhere close. Then we'll catch us up with Thursby.'

An evil smile appeared on Coburn's face. 'Now that's a meetin' I'm surely goin' to enjoy.'

'And one he won't be expectin'.'

They reached their quarry less than two hours later. It had been simple to pick out Thursby's route from his trail and to circle round in front of him.

Herne dismounted and lay along the upper slope of a bluff that overlooked the track the wagon was taking. Coburn waited further down and out of sight, mounted on his own horse and holding the reins of the grey they had chosen for Jed.

Herne's Sharps was nestled into his cheek and shoulder and he was watching with care the group riding eastwards. Thursby was sitting on the front of the wagon, alongside the driver. One rider was some twenty yards further ahead, an off-white hat pulled down over his eyes, a rifle diagonally across his saddle.

There were two men at the back, one of whom Herne recognized as Charlie Whitten.

The grey snickered and Coburn leaned across, placing his gloved hand to its mouth and murmuring gently. Herne focused on the white hat; it was a good target. From that angle the .55 calibre shell would smash through the top of the skull and drive through to the upper spine.

The finger on the trigger squeezed evenly: the hat was flattened at its crown: the horse shied sideways and reared up as first the man's rifle, then the man himself, crashed to the ground.

Herne pushed another shell up into the breech and trained the Sharps on the wagon driver.

Thursby shouted out in panic, then turned and yelled at the man next to him to get the horses moving fast. The driver raised his long whip and dropped it almost immediately as a bullet tore into the flesh between shoulder and side.

Herne sprang up and mounted his already moving horse.

As they rode down from the bluff, Whitten and his companion were alongside the wagon, shouting recriminations back and forth at the terrified Thursby.

The man to the right wheeled his mount round as he saw Herne and Coburn heading towards them. When he came out of the circle his pistol was drawn and up in front of his chest.

Coburn fired once and hit him in the hip; a second time and took him in the right forearm.

Whitten made no attempt to go for his gun. Thursby was not obviously armed. The two of them stared at their attackers tight-lipped.

Herne nodded at the driver and the wounded rider. 'You both had enough of this?'

They had.

'Get off'n that wagon and get over there. Make sure you ain't takin' any guns with you. You,' he gestured at the man who was swaying in his saddle, both hands to his shattered hip, 'you pull that rifle out of its bucket an' drop it to the ground. Then ride off out of here. One sight of you again an' we'll take your head right off your shoulders.'

The man glanced up the trail at the still form beside the white stetson. He knew that the man with greying hair wasn't fooling. He did just as he was told and rode slowly away.

'Mister Herne, I . . .'

'You shut your lyin' mouth, you half-breed bastard!' said Coburn, hatred clear in every line of his face. 'You just arranged for us to have us bushwhacked and backshot.'

'Gentlemen, I ne . . .'

Coburn was down from his horse in seconds. He jumped on to the wagon and his hands grabbed at Thursby's expensively tailored coat. He lifted him up and shook him as a dog would a rat. Then he threw him sideways to the ground and leapt down, legs straddling the small, frightened body.

Charlie Whitten sat motionless on his horse, his heart beating fast underneath his all-black garb, his gun untouched in its holster. The way he wanted it to stay. His left hand stayed well within Herne's sight – he didn't want to give the man a chance to kill him if he could avoid it.

'Pick him up, Whitey.'

Coburn did exactly that, pushing Thursby back against the side of the wagon. Thursby reached up with his right hand and steadied himself against the wooden planking. His dark eyes flickered from Herne to Coburn. It was the albino who terrified him most; he was the one he thought might take his life.

He was mistaken: he did not know that the man he had ordered killed back in the Laredo livery stable had been a friend of Herne's.

Not that it was possible to do anything about that now.

Herne moved his grey horse round so that his right side was nearest to the half-breed.

'The livery stable. Man worked there. Got himself killed. He get in your way?'

Thursby's mouth opened but no words came out. Herne repeated the question. Still no reply. Coburn took a pace towards him and raised his hand. Thursby blinked and spluttered.

'We ain't waitin' much longer.'

'He . . . it was his fault . . . we were driving the wagon out peaceful . . . there was no reason . . . he drew a gun . . . seized him and . . .' Thursby gulped in air. '. . . there was no way to keep him quiet . . . I didn't do it . . . one of the others . . . you've already killed him . . . it's over . . . you've . . .'

'You told him to do it?'

'No, I never . . .'

'You told him!' Herne's voice was more powerful, no longer questioning, but stating fact.

'I swear!' Thursby slumped down to his knees, hands raised in front of his chest as though in prayer. 'I swear to you I never ordered it done. I didn't want him killed, I . . .'

Words broke into a series of sobs and convulsions. The clasped hands shook wildly, the tears ran down the dark face. Thursby's whole body was torn by fear.

'I . . . I . . . no . . . no!'

'You're a lying, thievin' bastard!'

Herne drew his gun deliberately and shot the half-breed through the centre of his forehead. The skin stretched open and the bone splintered and split. Blood sprang suddenly outwards, as from a well.

As Thursby's body fell slowly sideways. Herne holstered his Colt. 'The man you had killed was a friend of mine.'

Charlie Whitten still hadn't moved. But he knew that his chances of getting away were getting more remote every second. If they'd been for letting him go, he would have been sent off with the others.

'What you aimin' to do with me?' he asked.

Coburn looked at him sharply. 'Depends on you.'

'Oh, I'll ride on out of here and never say nothin', you can depend on that.' His voice came fast and flustered.

Coburn only grinned. 'That weren't how I meant it. Not exactly.'

Whitten said nothing, just watched and waited.

Coburn stepped round him. 'That gun of yorn. Reckon you're really somethin' with that, huh?'

Whitten shrugged his shoulders. 'Maybe. I mean, I handle myself pretty well. I . . .'

'Get down off'n that horse.'

'But . . .'

'Get down!'

Whitten did as he was told. Herne had moved to the rear of the wagon, watching Coburn arrange his play. He had no intention of interfering.

'Now get yourself back down the trail a piece.'

Whitten's face twisted up to one side. 'What for? What you gonna do?'

Coburn smiled. 'Call yourself a gunfighter don't you?'

Whitten mumbled something neither Coburn nor Herne could hear.

'If you ain't, what you doin' goin' round totin' a gun that way and sellin' yourself to slime like that?' Coburn jerked a finger down at Thursby's dead body.

Herne came forward. 'Better do like he says. Seems to me you're gettin' a better chance than most.'

Charlie Whitten raised a hand to his cheek in an attempt to quell his nerves. He began to back away, eyes fixed on Whitey Coburn all the time. Longer strides now, left arm pushed out at an angle. A tall man in a black shirt and black pants who knew that if he could get the gun at his side up and into action fast enough he might save his life.

*If* he were fast enough.

'That's far enough, Charlie!'

Coburn was braced ready; legs apart, the rest of his body dropped forward into a gunfighter's crouch, right hand hovering above the butt of his Colt. His pink eyes watching the movement of Whitten's left arm, waiting for the dive downwards and into the arc of death.

Whitten was drenched in sweat, drops of it running down both sides of his face, glistening on the bridge of his nose. He flexed the fingers of his gun hand, praying that something would happen to make it all unnecessary. Knowing that it wouldn't.

A watch ticked off seconds deep inside his head, delaying what could no longer be delayed. He knew he had to make his play first to have any chance at all.

Now!

Coburn licked up at his top lip as his mouth opened slightly and his right hand went into action. Whitten's fear gave him an extra inch of speed. His pistol was pulled clear of its holster and began to come level.

That was when the first shot hit him plumb in the centre of the chest. He leapt back several feet but managed to keep his balance. His arm faltered then tried once more.

Coburn levered back the hammer of his .45 and took his time.

This time the shell went in higher and to the right, close to the heart. Whitten spun through a full circle, dropping to his knees at the end of it. Miraculously the fingers of his left hand kept their grip on the gun.

Dimly he heard the triple click through the waves of mist that befogged his brain. He lifted his head and saw the figure of the man with long white hair; a figure that appeared to be moving from side to side, swaying, swaying . . .

There was the sound of a single shot: fingers loosed their hold: life also.

Coburn holstered his Colt and turned to Jed. 'For a no account bastard, he weren't too bad when it came to it.'

Herne nodded. 'Guess we'll check the load some, then move on our way. Sooner I see New Orleans the better.'

They reopened the top crates. Thursby was slippery enough to have removed some of the stuff and stashed it away somewhere. But everything seemed to be as before.

The other crates had not been tampered with.

'Let's get 'em back on.'

Coburn bent over and took something in his hand.

'Jed!'

His shout was urgent and Herne whirled round fast, Colt coming up as he did so. He saw the statue flying towards him and threw up his left hand at the last moment, catching and holding it at the second attempt.

Coburn was squatting on his thin haunches, laughing loudly and slapping his knee. 'Damn me, Jed, you surely did look worried.'

Herne let his gun fall back into place and looked at the small, heavy statue, weighing it in both hands. 'You stupid bastard! We just risked our necks tryin' to keep this stuff and you go and throw it around.'

Coburn slapped his leg again and laughed all the more.

Pretty soon, Herne was laughing along with him.

## Chapter Eleven

The sun glowed from the mid-morning sky like a ball of slow-burning gold. Molten light reflected down on to the rooftops, turning the white of the still-lingering frost to a warm orange.

Here, close to the centre of New Orleans, the buildings were of brick, the sidewalk paved. Men and women went about their business smartly dressed, ignoring the two men passing through with their battered and dirty wagon. They were well used to trade: it was the foundation of the wealth of their city.

Herne edged his horse to the side of the street and leant down from the saddle. A man wearing a light grey suit and a dark grey hat looked up at him in surprise.

'We're lookin' for a place called Lacey Street. You know where that is?'

The man looked away from Herne and stroked his chin thoughtfully. 'It seems familiar. In name only. It is not a section of the city that I frequent.'

'All we want to know is how to get there and make a delivery.' Herne nodded back towards Coburn and the wagon.

'Well, sir, if you go down here for another two blocks, then left for another three. That will bring you to Canal Street. Left again on Canal Street and proceed right to the end. Lacey Street is thereabouts. At least, as far as I recall it is.'

Herne went over the directions again, while the man backed slowly away, anxious to be about his business.

'Thanks, anyway,' Herne finished and moved back to the wagon.

'Friendly sort, ain't they.' Whitey observed.

'Reckon they're friendly enough if'n you got money to spend. You an' me, we don't look like we got too much of nothin'.'

Coburn shook his head in agreement. 'Seems to me that's the way it's mostly been.' He looked up at Jed. 'Happen after today things'll be different.'

'Maybe you're right. Let's go and find Toomey and get rid of this stuff an' get us the rest of our money. I sure ain't anxious to stick around New Orleans a sight longer than I can help.'

'That's right.'

As they moved their load along the street a small boy wearing a clean blue and white sailor suit stared at them from the sidewalk. He pulled at his mother's skirts and when she inclined her elegant head towards him his voice was both excited and mystified.

'Mama! Mama! Who are those two old men with guns? Who are they?'

'Ssh, Daniel,' said his mother hastily, 'they're nobody.'

And she hurried him on his way.

The brick had given way to wood and broken glass. The streets were littered with rubbish and pitted with holes. In the corner of an old wagon that had been upended and abandoned, a mangy black cat licked at some anonymous pool of liquid. The knots of its spine showed clearly through the fur of its arched back.

From the open doors of warehouse buildings, the stink of rotted vegetables and fruit reached out to them and assailed their nostrils. By one of the cracked doors a large, fat rat feasted itself on a pile of decomposing garbage.

In that part of New Orleans, the rats lived better than the cats.

'God damn it, Jed! If this ain't the most stinkin' hole I ever bin in!'

'Damned right, Whitey.'

'I can't wait to get me out of this rotten city an' back into some fresh air. Somewheres a man can breath decent. Not this festerin' . . .'

'There she is,' interrupted Herne.

The street sign had fallen away and in its place someone had untidily daubed the name in paint: Lacy Streat, it read.

The building they were looking for lay close to the end of the street. Floyd Toomey and Partner, Importers and Exporters. Coburn hauled in the horses and tied the rein ends around the long brake handle. Herne got down from his grey and stood outside, looking at the flaking green paint on doors and walls. It sure didn't give the same impression that Toomey's clothes had.

Coburn pointed upwards: 'That there where it says "and Partner", you reckon that meant Thursby?'

'Could be.'

'Maybe someone ought to climb up there and put a line through that last part. A thick black line.'

Herne went to the sagging double doors and pushed at their centre. They swung back with a groan, the bottom of one scraping against the stone floor.

Herne's own faint shadow fell across the opening.

'Anyone around?' he called into the space.

No answer.

He unbuttoned his coat and pulled the right flap back behind the butt of his gun.

'Cover me,' he said to Coburn. 'I ain't about to take no chances at this stage.'

'Right.'

Herne stepped between the doors and into comparative darkness. Coburn came slowly up behind.

'Toomey! You there?'

Nothing.

Herne took another two steps forward and waited, allowing his eyes to become accustomed to the light. Soon he was able to make out the shape of steps going up to the left of what was a cavernous space. Above him and to the right, there appeared to be a kind of loft which ran along two sides. Opposite, at ground level, there were a few large packing cases randomly stacked. What looked like straw was strewn over the floor by the foot of the stairs. The place stank of disuse . . . and something worse, something indefinable.

There was a sudden scampering of movement from the midst of the straw and Herne's hand went to his gun. Whatever it was scurried across the warehouse and disappeared into the furthest corner.

The outlines of the place were thickening out. Above the flight of wooden steps, there was a square box-like room, from which a cat-walk led to the loft.

'It don't look like anyone's home,' said Coburn.

As the last word was uttered both men heard clearly the sound of a rifle being levered ready for action. Coburn ducked back against one side of the door. Herne moved fast to the wall opposite the steps, his body ducked low. They both had their guns drawn and cocked.

'Whoever it is up there, you better let that rifle alone and get where we can see you,' said Herne clearly and firmly.

All the two men could see was a shadow at the head of the steps.

'Why don't you drop your own weapons and show your arses to the daylight?' replied the shadow.

Herne made no answer, but kept his Colt trained on the shape above him. Coburn moved stealthily sideways, heading for the steps. The stink of the warehouse seemed worse each time he breathed.

'You hear what I said?' came the voice. 'You drop them guns and get out of here before I blow your damned heads off.'

From underneath the steps, Coburn could see the man's legs through a gap between the planking. He raised his pistol slowly.

'I ain't foolin' now. You shift yourselves or I'll let you have it where you stand.'

Coburn's voice came slow, but it came with an edge like the blade of a well-honed knife. 'That ain't nothin' to what you'll get if'n I squeeze down on this trigger a mite more. Reckon I'll blow your balls right off and ruin your digestion all in the same shot.'

They heard the man gulp in air.

'Throw down the rifle!' called Herne. 'Now!'

There was only a second's hesitation before the weapon rose up from the shadows and landed noisily on the stone floor.

'Now get yourself down them steps – and keep your hands high where we can both see 'em.'

The man who stepped gingerly down towards where Herne and Coburn were waiting was of medium height and build. He had sandy hair and was wearing a patch over his left eye. He could have been any age between thirty and fifty. The good eye blinked at Herne and blinked several times more when he saw Coburn.

'Who the hell are you? What you want round here anyways?'

'We're lookin' for Toomey.'

The man shook his head. 'Won't find him here. You'd better try some place else.'

Coburn moved towards him. 'What's his name doin' up outside then?'

'That. Well, he owns the place right enough. Never comes down here, though. Ain't seen him for weeks, months even.'

His gnarled hands were pushing and pulling at his belt as though frightened his pants might fall down at any moment.

Herne nodded in the direction the man had come from. 'Anyone else up there?'

'No. Just me.'

Coburn took the man's nose between finger and thumb hand and squeezed it tightly, pressing through to the bone beneath. 'You wouldn't be lyin' now, would you?'

The man tried to shake his head from side to side. 'Nope. Only me. Work here keepin' things in order for Mr. Toomey.'

Coburn sniffed. 'Don't seem you work at it hard.'

'You know where Toomey is?' Herne asked.

Coburn let go his grip. The impression of his fingers was indented clearly on the man's nose. The man nodded.

'Where?'

'Got an office near centre of the city. Lawyering. That's what he does. Most the time. This is more like a sideline with him. I can tell you how to get there right enough.'

He looked at Herne expectantly.

'That ain't the way I see it. We'll wait here while you go and fetch Toomey here.'

'But I can't do that, I . . .'

He cut himself short, seeing Jed Herne's expression harden, knowing that Coburn might get hold of him again at any moment.

'I'll go get my coat an' . . .'

'You get goin' right now. We don't want to stay in this stinkin' hole no longer than we must.'

The man turned to the doors. At the entrance he swung back. 'Suppose Mr. Toomey says he ain't coming? What then?'

'Just tell him it's Jed Herne who's got some things all the way from Mexico for him. He'll likely come then.'

The man nodded and stepped through into the light of the street. They heard the sound of his footsteps shuffling away and then it was quiet again.

'We sure don't have to wait in here, do we?' asked Whitey.

'Don't see why. 'Sides, I want to see Toomey as soon as he sees us – if not sooner.'

It was less than three quarters of an hour before Floyd Toomey arrived at the top end of Lacey Street. He was being driven in a carriage drawn by two black horses whose coats shone in the golden light of the sun. Gold but lacking in warmth.

The man who had been in the warehouse was driving the rig and two other men rode alongside. They wore guns at their hips and gave every impression of knowing how to use them.

Herne and Coburn climbed down from the wagon and stood close to the sidewalk, watching for any sign of trouble.

Toomey smile from his seat and waved a plump hand in their direction. He was as smartly dressed as at their previous meeting – and as fat. Whatever business he got his money from, it surely was treating him handsomely.

'Gentlemen! Gentlemen!' The voice greeted them loudly as soon as the driver reined the black horses to a halt.

He beamed down on them as though they were old friends. The men with him said and did nothing, apart from watch the two strangers with a mixture of apprehension and distaste. Without doubt the warehouse guard had told them what had happened earlier.

Toomey climbed awkwardly down from the rig, his bulk obstructing his progress. He brushed his hands down the front of his blue suit and then offered one to Herne and Coburn in turn.

They both looked at the large white hand and the inches of laced cuff on the wrist but did not move to shake it.

'Er, well, well, gentlemen. It is good to clap eyes on you both, nonetheless. On the pair of you and the, er . . .'

The eyes looked greedily past Herne and Coburn towards the wagon.

'This is the shipment, I presume?'

'Sure,' said Herne. 'Sure we got it. Just about.'

His expression took on a look of troubled amazement.

'You don't mean to say that the transaction took place with – er – difficulty?'

''Pends what you call difficult.'

'Well, I . . .'

Some men had come out of another warehouse higher on the street and were loitering nearby, openly listening to the conversation. Any activity in that run-down part of town attracted more than its fair share of attention.

'Gentlemen,' said Toomey quickly, 'let us step inside where others cannot overhear what we are saying. I have found it serves a man well to keep his affairs as close to his chest as possible.'

I'll just bet you have, thought Herne as he followed the fat man into the warehouse, I'll bet you have.

'Let's have some light in here,' said Toomey and one of his men fetched a hurricane lamp from the upstairs room and lit it, hanging the metal handle from a hook set into the loft floor.

The light spread round the room, casting long shadows on the wall.

'Now, sir,' said Toomey to Herne, 'you were mentioning difficulties.'

'Seems the Mexicans thought you arranged to give 'em twice what you sent us down there with. We had to shoot our way out.'

Toomey looked properly bewildered. 'Gentlemen – er – I assure you my side of the bargain was fairly kept. The sellers of this merchandise were trying to get more than their agreed due. You have my word on that.'

Herne nodded, wondering just how much that word was worth. He noted that the stench of the building was now threaded through with the sickly sweet smell of the lawyer's perfume. How in hell's name could you trust a man who put stuff like that on his hair and body?

'That partner of yorn,' said Coburn from the edge of the circle of light, 'he still workin' with you?'

Toomey didn't even blink before answering. 'Sir, that is one of the strangest things to have happened. Some days ago we were due to meet in my office. Antonio Thursby never showed up. No reason. No excuse. Nobody in New Orleans has seen hide nor hair of him since.'

He finished the statement with a wide gesture of his hands, rings glinting dully and in strange contrast to the grease and filth now even more evident upon the floor.

Coburn cleared his throat and spat through the partly open doors. Herne said quietly, 'You ain't about to see nothin' of him, either.'

Toomey appeared surprised. 'What, sir, you know something of what has happened to the man?'

Herne thought that one of Toomey's hired men was starting to get restless, his hands fidgeting at his gun belt. He stared at the man for a moment before answering.

'Not something. Everything. He's dead. Bullet in his head.'

Toomey took half a pace backwards and rested a hand ostentatiously on his spreading stomach.

'How can you be sure of that, Mr. Herne?'

Herne allowed his right hand to rest on the butt of his Colt; he did it slowly, clearly. It wasn't a gesture he wanted any of them to miss.

'I know 'cause it was me put the bullet there.'

The interior of the warehous was suddenly very still. It was as if all six men were holding their breath. The only sound that of a scuffling in the rubbish outside the brightest light. The only sign of what Floyd Toomey might be thinking showing in the nerve that began to twitch underneath one cheek.

Then that, too, was brought under control.

Toomey's voice had lost some of its former resonance. 'I am sure, sir, that you had every good reason for taking such an action.'

'Damn right I did! He tried to pay me off an' take over

the load. I didn't take to that none. One thing, it wasn't our agreement. For another, I reckoned as he might be cheatin' on you.' Herne paused and looked Toomey straight in the face. 'You didn't send him out to meet us, did you?'

'No, sir, indeed I did not. This whole aspect of the affair comes as a great surprise to me. A very great surprise.'

'That's all right then. 'Cause it was when he tried to get the stuff from us by force that we killed him – and most of them he had with him.'

The last speaker was Whitey Coburn, his voice hard and flat, almost as though he were pushing the fat lawyer as far as he could. Urging a reaction. Knowing that if there were to be a showdown then the sooner it came the better.

But there was nothing.

Nothing but the foul smell of the building laced with Toomey's expensive perfume. That and the man himself smiling and saying to the pair of them: 'That being the case gentlemen, I am – er – more than grateful that you should have done me such a service. Thursby was obviously more wretched than I had even begun to suspect.'

He clasped Herne's shoulders and smiled widely. 'When we are working out the bonus we spoke of before, the matter of Antonio Thursby will be taken into account.' He stepped away again and included Coburn in his glance. 'Indeed it will.'

Herne was anxious to take the lawyer at his word and get out as soon as possible. But the fat man insisted that they first examine the merchandise. He instructed two of his men to get the wagon into the warehouse so that it could be unloaded.

'It will not take us long, gentlemen, after which we shall – er – terminate our little business together. Yes, very satisfactorily, too.'

The men began to lift the crates down and Toomey asked Herne if he and Coburn would mind assisting them. After all, it would get everything finished that much more quickly.

The two agreed and joined in with the task of stacking and checking the contents.

There was a loud crack as one of the crates was dropped on to its end by Toomey's men. He stormed into the centre of the warehouse, arms waving excitedly, his voice higher and louder then before.

'Damn you! You incompetent fools! Don't you realize that what you are handling is precious and easily breakable? There are untold treasures inside those boxes and if you are careless with them now when I have succeeded in getting them this far . . .!'

The man who had dropped the box scowled and looked away. Herne and Coburn exchanged a quick glance, a wry grin crossing Whitey's face. He was thinking back to when he had thrown the statue and Jed had only just managed to catch hold of it.

Herne realized what Whitey was thinking about and smiled back at him. The fuss Toomey was making, it would serve him right if some of the junk *was* broken.

They carried on with the work, bending over the wooden crates and extracting the objects carefully. The straw was thrown to the floor and Toomey made his massive way round the warehouse, beaming as he accepted each new find into his large, sweaty hands.

Coburn coughed and hawked up a mouthful of dark yellow phlegm. 'Jesus Christ!' he exclaimed to Herne, 'I shall be a damned sight happier when we can get us out of this stinkin' hole and back into some open range. A blow of fresh wind through these lungs of mine 'd make me feel a sight better.'

'Still hankerin' after that place of your own down by some peaceful river?' asked Herne, smiling.

'You bet I am! First thing I'm goin' t' do when this is over is ride out and find me just the place I'm lookin' for. Ain't goin' t' waste another minute. Seems to me I wasted too much damned time already.'

Jed Herne nodded and looked round as Toomey gasped with delight at a bowl one of his men had handed to him. He noticed that the man with the patch had moved away from the crates and was standing halfway up the steps, his rifle back in his hand.

Toomey was turning the brown and red bowl round and round in one hand, marvelling at its workmanship. To Herne, it still didn't look like it was worth thousands of dollars. He certainly couldn't understand why Thursby had been so willing to kill to get his hands on it all.

He looked at the statue in his right hand. Dark and ill-formed. Heavy.

He grinned suddenly and looked at Whitey bending over one of the crates, sideways on to Herne himself. Herne swung back his arm and shouted.

'Whitey!'

The albino jerked round as Herne threw the statue high through the space between them. Toomey saw it go and called out in alarm. Coburn's hand had already begun the movement towards his gun. Too late he realized that Jed had turned the tables on him. In vain he tried to release his Colt and catch the statue.

It bounced up off the back of his left hand, on to the palm of his right; once, then a second time; then down on to the stone floor.

It shattered on impact, the brittle surface splitting apart and revealing a sudden spray of uncut diamonds sparkling in the light of the hurricane lamp.

## Chapter Twelve

For a frozen moment nobody moved. All stared down at the bright glitter of wealth in the centre of the grime and dirt stunned by what had happened.

Then everyone was pulling at his gun and taking off for whatever cover the place afforded.

From the stairs, the man with the patch fired once in the general direction of Herne. As the bullet ricocheted at a crazy angle off the stone floor, Herne drew his Colt and shot through the glass of the hurricane lamp. There was a splintering sound and the flame leapt and flickered, but refused to die.

More shots sounded hollowly in the high room. Guns were being fired without aim or thought, in a frenzy of panic. Toomey was shouting out instructions to his men, but the words were lost in the rest of the noise.

Coburn had made a run for the stairs, ducking under the blow that had been aimed at him with the rifle and pushing the man with the patch from the steps to the floor. He dived low on the cat-walk as someone below fired upwards twice.

Toomey was still yelling, though by now he was in the shadows at the far side of the warehouse. Herne had crouched low behind a couple of crates and was waiting for the initial burst of shooting to die down.

The lamp was still swinging from its nail, casting weird shadows from those antiquities that had been uncovered.

Uncovered and now partly shot to pieces, gold and diamonds spilling from their hollows.

Hearne leaned his gun barrel on the top of one of the crates and aimed for the lamp's base. The shell went through it and embedded itself in the floor of the loft. Oil began to pour downwards in a steady stream. The flame rose up with a final, orange burst of bowed light, then guttered to nothingness.

The warehouse was now in total darkness.

The only source of light was the crack in the double doors that had been slammed shut with the weight of a man's body.

The oil continued to drip to the floor: that and the heavy breathing of men the only sounds.

Herne moved his left hand and felt it slide into something damp and sticky to the touch. He pulled the hand away and wiped it on his pants. In the spaces before him he could see nothing definite; nothing to aim at.

Coburn had made no move.

Herne leaned his body the other way, trying to get a firm grip on a crate. That ought to stir things up a little!

He started to lift it from the ground as noiselessly as possible, but the bottom edge scraped on the floor. After that it was a case of moving fast. Herne rocked back on his haunches, raising the crate level with his head before hurling it down into the centre of the warehouse.

As it crashed on to the stone and bounced back upwards, the wooden sides cracked and broke apart, spilling out the contents.

'There he is!' Toomey's shout seemed to come from the deepest recess of the vast room.

A volley of shots rang out from three different directions, all aimed at the area where the crate had landed. Herne had been waiting, not wishing to waste his moment.

He aimed for the middle one of the trio of flashes and

cursed to himself when there was no resulting cry of pain or sound of a body falling. He had aimed well he was sure. The man must have been firing left handed; his shot had been intended for the chest of someone firing with his right.

He wouldn't make the same mistake next time.

And there was still nothing from Coburn.

'Did you get either of them?' Toomey's voice echoed round the walls and finally faded. There was no reply.

Moments more silence and then to Herne's left a muffled shout, followed closely by a scream and a gurgling cry.

'What the hell?' Floyd Toomey was unused to asking so many unanswered questions, but the thump of a body falling heavily told Herne that Whitey had not been wasting his time.

It was time he made his next move. Like drawing a little more fire. He pulled another crate up into his arms and brought it higher than before, so that he was now standing. If he could get this one across towards the far side, that would likely give Whitey and himself a good sighting.

He took a step forward and his right foot slid away under him, skidding on the greasy floor. The crate went from his grasp and fell directly down, banging loudly and breaking open. Almost instantly came Toomey's shout and a swift succession of shots.

Herne couldn't stifle his gasp of pain as one of them tore at the flesh of his side, going through coat and shirt and skin to graze the outside of his ribs. He fell to his left, snapping off a shot as he did so.

Without balance there was little chance of hitting anyone and the shell was wasted. Whitey didn't seem to have had any better luck.

'You got the bastard! Let him have it now while he's on the floor!' Toomey's voice was much louder, closer, more triumphant.

Herne pulled at the uneven flagstones with his finger ends, till a bullet struck the floor inches in front of them. He changed direction fast, pushing himself back towards the middle of the warehouse despite the waves of pain that swept through him.

He crashed his legs against a pile of packing materials and pots, sending them flying.

'There he is!'

The shot was followed by a violent burst of flame from directly beside where Herne was now lying. He had made his way back to where the pool of oil had spread itself: the pool that had finally caught alight.

'That'll finish him!'

Toomey's voice seemed to be coming from behind and above him and from its gloating tone, Herne knew who had thrown the matches down into the oil.

He glimpsed Whitey's anxious face on the far side of the circle of fire and even as he did so, a second shell struck him in the right side, lower than the first. He flung up his right hand, fingers apart. The Colt tumbled out of his grasp and clanged on to the floor.

'Finish him! Finish him!'

Coburn fired once at the man with the patch and didn't wait to see if his shot had been accurate. He had to get Jed out of there. He put his left arm in front of his face and ran at the flames, which were now burning higher, fueled by the straw and wood that lay all around the building.

'I'm comin', Jed!'

He leapt through the fire and as he did so two shots rang out from in front and behind. The first took him low in the stomach, inches above his left hip. The second smashed into the corner of his right shoulder blade and glanced upwards through the top of his neck.

He threw his arms out wide, spreadeagled on the wall of flame.

Herne looked up from the floor and saw Whitey's white, stricken face, white hair splayed out around it. And about that bright orange flame.

He was staring at the angel of death.

Coburn fell inside the fire and Herne grabbed at him with his left hand, up on his knees now and trying to recover his gun at the same time. He pulled it up with him, side and arm coursing with streaks of pain as he levered back the hammer.

He stepped through the smoke and dragged Whitey with him.

One of Toomey's men was outlined against the opening between the doors. Herne fired once and grunted with satisfaction as the body plummetted forwards and stayed where it had fallen. He lowered Coburn to the floor and got into the street as fast as he could.

The man with the patch was sitting in Toomey's rig, trying to whip up the horses for a getaway. Where he was going he wasn't going to need horses.

Herne winced as he squeezed the trigger twice, hitting the man in the upper arm and then in the side of the head, knocking him clean out of the rig.

The horses bolted, taking the empty carriage along Lacey Street at great speed. But of their owner, of Floyd Toomey, there was neither sight nor sound.

Herne went back into the warehouse and pulled Coburn out into the street. The blood was welling from the wound in Whitey's neck and a dark stain was spreading fast at the front of his shirt.

Jed put his left arm under Whitey's head and raised it up.

'Take it easy. I'll fetch a doc.'

Whitey shook his head, the eyes already glazed, their pupils contracting. His voice was a faint croak so that Herne had to bend low over him.

'Are . . . you . . . all r . . . right?'

'Sure. Thanks to you.'

'And the ones . . aaahh! . . . ones . . . who . . . oohh!'

Herne looked away, then back down at Whitey's face. 'I finished 'em. Don't worry.'

Whitey started to lift his hand upwards, its fingers

clenched tightly around something. He lifted it in front of Herne's face and opened it slowly, his face contorting with the effort. A handful of gold dust lay in the palm of his hand, along with the dirt of the warehouse floor.

He looked at the gold and then at Jed and tried to smile but it was only another grimace of extreme pain. 'At . . . at least . . . I got it . . . part right . . .'

The fingers opened wider; the hand shook with a final spasm; the gold dust trickled between the fingers of the dying man's hand like the sands of time.

Herne felt the body shake under him and then all there was left was a flower of blood blossoming around his mouth and a pair of dead eyes staring at some land Herne did not know and could only imagine.

He rested Whitey's head back on the pavement and gently lowered his eyelids.

There was nothing more he could do.

Then.

Jed Herne knew there was no hurry. He found himself a small boarding house and took a room for two weeks which he rarely left except to eat his meals in the long dining-room with the other lodgers. The doctor came to see him every day for the first week, changing the dressings on his wounds and making sure they were healing up the way they should.

After that it was a matter of resting and regaining his strength. Time spent in front of the full-length wardrobe mirror testing his right arm; reaching for his Colt and thumbing back the hammer.

Time after time until he was certain.

Only then did he pay his rent and step out once more into the streets of New Orleans.

He went first to the railroad station and inquired about the trains to New York. He paid a deposit on the ticket, using all of the money he had left. That didn't worry him none either. He knew he was about to collect his dues.

The clerk in front of Floyd Toomey's office tried to hold out on the tall gunfighter – but not for long. One glimpse of the bayonet blade sliding up from inside the man's boot was enough.

Herne grunted and left for Bourbon Street.

The Bourbon Sporting House was almost exactly halfway down, a brightly painted sign outside advertising its wares. The best girls, the best gaming tables, the best steaks in New Orleans.

A negro doorman looked up inquiringly at Herne and began to mumble a question. He saw the determination on Herne's face and didn't bother finishing it. He was just mighty glad that whoever or whatever the stranger was looking for, it wasn't him.

The room into which Herne stepped was richly furnished with purple and gold velvet drapes and long, low sofas upholstered in the same material. Upon these a number of strikingly beautiful women sat or lay, wearing a variety of underthings in shiny, coloured satin. Satin which shimmered over the curves of their bodies as they moved.

One of them slid from the end of an elegant chaise-longue and came towards Herne. She walked with a sway of the hips and a tilt of the head that gave her the sensuous aristocracy of a queen.

A queen cat on heat.

She was an octoroon and as she opened her full lips in a smile, Herne was struck by the orange aroma of her perfume. Her cheeks were rouged, the dark eyes made up strongly but not overpoweringly.

Herne thought back to the whore he had had back in that Mexican cantina. This one was in a class of her own; so much more beautiful. The thought of going with her to her bed filled him with a momentary shiver of excitement.

She stood before him, her smile half-mocking now, her voice warm and smooth. 'There hasn't been a man like you in here for a long time. I surely hope you ain't about to go off with anybody else. Not while I'm here.'

She fluttered her false eyelashes and rested a hand on his arm, the long, crimson nails pressing down insistently on his flesh.

'I can give you more pleasure than anyone.'

The beautiful face rose up towards him.

'I can do things you never even dreamed about.'

Herne was swimming in her perfume and the dusky warmth of her closeness. The hand gripped him and her lips reached up towards his mouth.

Herne stepped back, releasing the fingers from his arm. Instantly the expression on her face changed.

'I'm lookin' for someone,' he said. 'A man.'

She looked at him quizzically. 'Well, if that's your taste, you'd . . .'

'A man named Toomey. Floyd Toomey. You know him?'

The face hardened further and the girl turned away and began to walk back to where she had been sitting. Herne went after her and stopped her with a hand on her shoulder.

She wheeled round and swung her hand hard at his face, slapping him across the cheek.

The crack of the blow served to halt most of the surrounding noise. Talking, drinking ceased. The Negro pianist struck another half a dozen syncopated notes and left them to reverberate in the warmth of the room.

Herne rubbed at his cheek, his other hand still tight on the octoroon's shoulder.

'Let her go, mister!'

Herne tried to judge the voice but was left uncertain. Man or woman?

'Let her go and back off afore I fill your back with both of these barrels.'

Herne took his hand from the girl's shoulder and turned slowly, tensing his body for action.

The shotgun was levelled at him from the top of three plushly carpeted steps. The person who was holding it was dressed like a man but Herne didn't think it was. Something about the build, the face, the voice, suggested a woman.

A dark brown suit which swelled out at the chest below a white carnation in the buttonhole. Short, fair hair. A face without makeup but with an oddly feminine mouth.

It didn't matter. The finger on the trigger was real enough, strong enough.

'No one comes in here and manhandles my girls. No one!'

The legs widened their stance, the gun was pulled in more tightly against the body.

'You get right out of here and don't come back.'

Herne said nothing. Merely shook his head.

The gun jerked in his direction. 'I said you get! Or else get this!'

'Got me business here. I aim to see it done.'

'And I aim to see you dead for it!'

Herne's eyes narrowed; the fingers of his right hand flexed. 'Don't make me do it.'

But there was to be no going back.

Herne went for his gun and ducked low at the same time. The fingers round the shotgun trigger tightened as he fired. As his shell struck home the shotgun exploded both barrels over the top of where Herne had been standing.

The weapon fell away and bounced down the steps on to the floor. Herne's bullet had penetrated her breast and severed the artery close to the heart. She landed face downwards and the blood from her body seeped into the thick pile of the carpet.

All around Herne women were screaming at the tops of their voices; men shouting and cursing. A group rushed through from the neighbouring gaming room and yelled for an explanation.

Several prominent citizens of the city ran for the door, pulling on their clothes as they went.

Herne turned suddenly at a movement in the corner of his vision. By the gaming room door a man in a striped shirt and fancy waistcoat was releasing a deringer from its holster just behind his hip.

Herne thumbed back the hammer and brought round the gun. He fired once, taking his time. The gambler rocked back against the door jamb, a playing card fluttering down from inside his shirt sleeve.

He moved his hand towards the wound high in his chest but the action was unfinished.

'Anybody else feel like chippin' in?'

Herne turned a slow, full circle, Colt primed and ready. There were no takers.

It was then that he noticed the girl.

She was on the floor behind where he had been standing. What was left of her. She had taken most of the force of both barrels of the shotgun. Her beautiful face was beautiful no longer. It hardly existed.

Where there had been fine bone structure, perfectly painted lips and eyes, now there was only a bloody pulp matted with hair and fragments of buckshot.

The upper half of her orange satin slip was stained deep, deep red.

Two of the other girls were kneeling alongside her mutilated body, holding each other and sobbing hysterically.

Herne straightened and looked above them. On the balcony which ran to the left of the single flight of stairs stood Floyd Toomey. His bulbous face was as pale as death itself, both hands gripping the silver painted rail until it shook.

Herne smiled a wry smile of satisfaction and began to climb the stairs.

'Which room, Toomey?'

The lips moved but were unable to speak; his eyes flickered like frightened birds. Herne followed his gaze and prodded him with his gun.

'Get movin'!'

Herne pushed the fat man into the room and shut the door. Almost immediately there was a movement underneath the mass of bedclothes. Herne jumped fast and pulled the sheets and blankets clear and on to the floor.

Two naked girls were huddled on the bare bed, one black, the other white. Neither looked older than fifteen.

'Get out!'

Herne reopened the door and locked it behind them. Then he put up his gun. He wasn't about to be in need of it.

Toomey was half sitting, half lying on the bed, his eyes tight shut as though it were a nightmare and he would wake up and it would all be over.

It would be over soon enough but he wasn't about to wake up.

Herne pulled him round and hit him full in the centre of his face. Blood spurted from the nose and Toomey lifted his arms instinctively. Herne kneed him in the stomach and then punched him in the face again. Harder. The nose splintered and broke under the impact of the blow.

'First I want the money!'

Toomey didn't even bother bluffing. He pulled a bulging wallet from inside his coat and let it fall on to the bed. All the while he was wincing and groaning with pain; the drops of blood that fell steadily from his face were patterning the yellow silk bed linen.

Herne took his and Whitey's due from the wallet, then counted out a thousand dollars more.

'That's the bonus you spoke of.'

The podgy hand reached for the wallet and what was left of the money. As the fingers closed around it, Herne reached down to his boot.

'Now there's one more payment you got to make.'

Toomey turned, startled, seeing the bayonet in Herne's hand.

'Whitey was my friend. A good and true friend. You sure can't pay enough for gettin' him killed, but sweet Jesus you can do your best!'

'Noooo!'

Floyd Toomey let out a high-pitched squeal and scrambled along the bed towards the far wall. Herne reached out for him with his left hand and jerked the fat body back into the centre of the bed. As feet and hands waved up into the air, the bayonet blade drove down hard into the squealing, wriggling centre.

'Aaahh! Aaahh!'

Herne slid the blade back through the excess of flesh. Then he pushed up the flabby chin and cut Toomey's throat from ear to ear in a single, sharp curving stroke.

Herne stood and looked down at the bed. He pulled the satin sheets over the body and watched the yellow change colour. A dead weight of flesh and bone wrapped in expensive whore house linen.

There was nothing more for Jed Herne to do.

It was a long journey from New Orleans north to New York. Long and cold. Herne spent much of it staring through the train windows, watching bayou change to open plain, plain to hills and back again. He fought to control his thoughts but it was difficult.

He saw the worn hands in front of him as they rested on his thighs, saw his reflection in the glass against the passing landscape. A face that seemed deeply lined, hair that hung past his shoulders and was greyer than he had noticed before.

In two days Becky would step down from the gangplank of the ship bringing her back from England. Back from a year in which she had finished her schooling. Had grown, perhaps, from a girl into a young woman.

Her mind and body matured.

Jed recalled the sudden touch of her lips upon his when she had bade him good-bye. No hand had been able to wipe that away.

And what would happen now?

How would they live, Becky and himself? Would their

lives continue to be bound together or would she build a life of her own, independent of him?

Half of Herne wished he could be without the responsibility of looking after her, caring for her as though she were his own daughter. The rest of him was jealous at the prospect of her becoming someone else's. Father or lover.

Herne stared through the window of the train once more. The lines of silver birches paraded themselves alongside the track, each one reflecting for an instant the flare of the orange sun.

Herne closed his eyes and the image of Whitey's stricken, dying face filled his mind.

He opened them and it was still there, outlined by a halo of flashing flame.

Herne cursed aloud and brought his clenched fist down hard on the table before him. He got up from his seat and went off to the buffet car in search of a bottle of whiskey. A bottle of Jim Beam in which to toast his friend's memory.

* * *

The sails of the ship fluttered like so many giant birds as they were reefed ready for coming into harbour. Jed Herne hunched his shoulders against the cold and pulled the hat down over his face. He leaned back against the wall at the end of the dock, keeping well clear of the others who also waited for their relatives and friends on their way from Europe.

Soon it was close enough for him to be able to pick out the name written about the prow, to see the slight figure of a girl leaning over the deck rail, looking as though she could scarcely wait for the ship to dock.

Herne glanced upwards as thick flakes of snow began suddenly to fall from out of the grey sky. He looked at the pale, searching face of the girl.

Winter had come and so had Becky.

THE END

## DOC LEROY, M.D. BY J. T. EDSON

Marvin Eldridge Leroy had been on the point of leaving home to attend medical college when bushwack lead cut down his parents. Although he was forced to abandon his plans and take a job as a cowhand, he never forgot his ambition of following in his father's footsteps and becoming a qualified doctor. Working on ranches, or driving cattle over the northbound trails to the Kansas railheads, he took every opportunity to continue his medical studies – and gradually he earned a reputation as a doctor . . . people even called him 'Doc'. There were men, women and children alive who would have been dead without his assistance. There were also men who had died at his hands – experience had made him lightning fast with a Colt . . .

0 552 10406 X 50p

## OLE DEVIL AT SAN JACINTO BY J. T. EDSON

In 1835, the oppressions of Presidente Antonio Lopez de Santa Anna had driven the colonists in Texas to rebellion. Major General Sam Houston, realizing that his small force could only hope to face the vast Mexican army when conditions were favourable, had ordered a tactical withdrawal to the east.

At last, on Thursday, April 21st, 1836, Houston decided that the time had come to make a stand. The Mexican Army, fifteen hundred strong, was on the banks of the San Jacinto river; Houston, with half that number, launched the attack that would decide the future of Texas.

0 552 10505 8 60p

## SACKETT'S LAND BY LOUIS L'AMOUR

My first realisation, after an immediate stab of fear, was that the Indians wore no paint. There were stories enough in England about Indians painting for war.

'Put your weapons out of sight,' I said, 'below the gunwhales. I think they are peaceful.' The canoes slowed their pace, gliding down to us, and then a hand lifted, palm outward, and I recognised Potaka. 'It is my friend' I explained.

Rufisco snorted, 'No Indian is your friend,' he said, 'Keep your gun handy.'

0 552 09849 3 40p

## THE CALIFORNIOS BY LOUIS L'AMOUR

Somewhere, in the mountains of California, there was gold. And the only man who knew where to find that gold was a strange old Indian, known as Juan . . . The Mulkerins were Irish – a fierce, proud and independant family. But through a run of bad luck they found themselves in the debt of Zeke Wooston – a hard, cruel man who was just waiting to take their ranch if they didn't pay up. It looked as though the Mulkerins were going to have to fight Zeke's gang and the Law – until Sean Mulkerin remembered the story of the gold . . . If only they could find the gold, their troubles would be over . . . but first they had to find Juan – and time was running out – fast . . .

0 552 09696 2 35p

## VIOLENCE AT SUNDOWN BY FRANK O'ROURKE

The town had been quiet for too long. Sooner or later there was bound to be violence in Olalla. A stray bullet and a dead cowpuncher were just the excuse two bitter men needed. The chance death gave them the reason to commit a vengeance killing . . . a reason to crush Marshal Bob Travis and the law he was pledged to uphold.

A tense Nebraska town splits wide open as a maddened range boss and his crafty foreman call the shots for VIOLENCE AT SUNDOWN.

0 552 10430 2 50p

## LATIGO BY FRANK O'ROURKE

The idea was fool proof. Addis planned the action, Brotherton set the stage, and Ellington faked the holdup. They'd made the getaway at night after meeting at the river and splitting the haul. Then it would be lights out for the unsuspecting Ellington . . .

But they hadn't reckoned on the storm that flattened Ellington – and the money – and delivered both into the hands of Hester Johnson, who lived like a man, loved like a woman, and never forgot a grudge.

0 552 10407 8 50p

# A SELECTED LIST OF CORGI WESTERNS FOR YOUR READING PLEASURE

J. T. EDSON

| | | | |
|---|---|---|---|
| ☐ | 10158 3 | **OLE DEVIL AND THE CAPLOCKS** | *J. T. Edson* 50p |
| ☐ | 08020 9 | **COMANCHE** | *J. T. Edson* 45p |
| ☐ | 08011 X | **THE BULL WHIP BREED** | *J. T. Edson* 45p |
| ☐ | 08017 9 | **THE COLT AND THE SABRE** | *J. T. Edson* 45p |
| ☐ | 07897 2 | **THE RIO HONDO KID** | *J. T. Edson* 45p |
| ☐ | 07892 1 | **TROUBLE TRAIL** | *J. T. Edson* 45p |
| ☐ | 08133 7 | **WAGONS TO BACKSIGHT** | *J. T. Edson* 45p |
| ☐ | 08195 7 | **THE MAN FROM TEXAS** | *J. T. Edson* 45p |
| ☐ | 08194 9 | **THE WILDCATS** | *J. T. Edson* 45p |
| ☐ | 08140 X | **THE PEACEMAKERS** | *J. T. Edson* 45p |
| ☐ | 08196 5 | **THE TROUBLEBUSTERS** | *J. T. Edson* 45p |

LOUIS L'AMOUR

| | | | |
|---|---|---|---|
| ☐ | 08650 9 | **KIOWA TRAIL** | *Louis L'Amour* 40p |
| ☐ | 09351 3 | **CONAGHER** | *Louis L'Amour* 40p |
| ☐ | 09350 5 | **THE LONELY MEN** | *Louis L'Amour* 40p |
| ☐ | 09343 2 | **DOWN THE LONG HILLS** | *Louis L'Amour* 40p |
| ☐ | 07815 8 | **MATAGORDA** | *Louis L'Amour* 40p |
| ☐ | 10231 8 | **OVER BY THE DRY SIDE** | *Louis L'Amour* 50p |

MORGAN KANE

| | | | |
|---|---|---|---|
| ☐ | 09425 0 | **DUEL IN TOMBSTONE** | *Louis Masterson* 35p |
| ☐ | 09467 6 | **TO THE DEATH, SENOR KANE!** | *Louis Masterson* 35p |
| ☐ | 09764 0 | **BLOODY EARTH** | *Louis Masterson* 30p |
| ☐ | 09794 2 | **NEW ORLEANS GAMBLE** | *Louis Masterson* 30p |
| ☐ | 09877 9 | **APACHE BREAKOUT** | *Louis Masterson* 35p |

SUDDEN

| | | | |
|---|---|---|---|
| ☐ | 08811 0 | **SUDDEN** | *Oliver Strange* 50p |
| ☐ | 09117 0 | **SUDDEN TAKES THE TRAIL** | *Oliver Strange* 60p |
| ☐ | 09118 9 | **THE LAW O'THE LARIAT** | *Oliver Strange* 60p |

*All these books are available at your bookshop or newsagent, or can be ordered direct from the publisher. Just tick the titles you want and fill in the form below.*

.................................................................................................................

**CORGI BOOKS,** Cash Sales Department, P.O. Box 11, Falmouth, Cornwall.

Please send cheque or postal order, no currency.

**U.K.** send 19p for first book plus 9p per copy for each additional book ordered to a maximum charge of 73p to cover the cost of postage and packing.

**B.F.P.O. and Eire** allow 19p for first book plus 9p per copy for the next 6 books thereafter 3p per book.

**Overseas Customers:** Please allow 20p for the first book and 10p per copy for each additional book.

NAME (Block letters)..........................................................

ADDRESS.................................................................................

(NOV 77) ................................................................................

While every effort is made to keep prices low, it is sometimes necessary to increase prices at short notice. Corgi Books reserve the right to show new retail prices on covers which may differ from those previously advertised in the text or elsewhere.